I0760579

THE SECOND BOOK OF NERO AND SPORUS

IMPERATRIX

S.P. SOMTOW

DIPLODOCUS PRESS · 2023

Imperatrix is the second volume of S.P. Somtow's trilogy *Nero and Sporus.* It originally appeared as a serial on Amazon Vella

ISBN: 978-1-940999-86-9

first published December 24, 2023

First Edition
published by Diplodocus Press
48 Sukhumvit 33 Bangkok 10110

printed and distributed by Amazon
410 Terry Ave. N Seattle, WA 98109 Or

ISBN:

0 9 8 7 6 5 4 3 2 1

I would like to dedicate this book
to the memory of
my father,
who was the first person
to try to teach me Latin

CONTENTS

IMPERATRIX

Cito fit quod dii volunt

When the Gods want something
It happens fast.

— Petronius

I

INSULTING THE GOD

Mistress of the World? You'll tell me what it felt like? But you've been silent for hours. And time is running out. I want to hear it all.

Don't ask me yet. You made me think of my first dominus, Petronius.

It becomes more painful now.

What do you mean? You've told me about being abducted from your village. About being broken in by a pirate, whipped by a tutor, raped by a senator. You've told me of the death of your master, a man you loved with all your heart, a death commanded by a tyrant. Those are tragic, are they not? Could anything be more painful?

Can you ask? You, who are one of the agents of my execution?

From the horrors of the slave market, you are going to step into a world of perfumed baths, oriental silks, lavish banquets, sitting at the apex of the known world. Surely the next chapter of your biography is sweeter than the last.

In fact, my story turns dark, and darker still. After all, I'm sitting here in chains. Not the heavy, clanking chains of a galley slaves, but delicate chains as befit the status I have fallen from. My throne is a make-up stool, my kingdom the Circus, and I'm unlikely to survive being raped in public by the God of Death.

And yet your time as Empress must have been a bright moment in your grim story.

A bright moment?

You're in in luck. A reprieve. The giraffes are revolting.

Revolting?

Against their trainers. They're in a panic. They're not like lions. People haven't had decades of experiencing in training giraffes for the arena, and the fact that their necks can reach the Imperial box is causing chaos. You hear the hubbub outside? They are restoring order. The games won't resume until the crowd is under control.

So I have more time to contemplate my doom.

I think of it as more time to hear your fascinating story.

Only if you can order a better grade of wine. Better yet, tell the guards to escort me to a proper toilet. You've had me in makeup all day already. The bucket is not only degrading, but lonely. Public defecation is more comforting. The coming and going. And the people of Rome, from aristocrat to pickpocket, all coming to the same level, all at their most vulnerable.

One of the things I missed, when I was Empress.

Sharing a sponge on a stick with a senator, a baker, and a male whore from the suburra?

The public lavatories are the single remaining bastion of the Republic.

***

As the litter moved toward the Palatine, I did not even dare pull back the curtain. Marcus Vinicius was walking alongside. I didn't want to see his face. Or anyone's face. I clutched Petronius's letter to my chest. It meant my death, for certain, but then again, what life did I have anyway?

Fortunately, Marcus left me in silence.

We had left Petronius's home at the fifth hour, and the day was growing warmer. Each step up the Palatine increased my unease.

Seeing Himself isn't a question of just turning up and being announced. There are barriers of being vetted and searched. But today, I was just waved through, thanks perhaps to Marcus. Or perhaps not. The guards seemed anxious, nervous, even; and I knew it could not have anything to with the suicide of my patronus.

Marcus still walked with me and I asked him what was going on.

"You'll see," was all he said.

The walk to the presence of Himself is designed to be intimidating. You saw him in marble before you saw him in the flesh. Walking down a cloister, the face of Himself peered down from an inner wall, from a garden. The face was idealized, made as godlike as possible. The statues were painted in colors brighter than reality; the world of the gods is more vivid than our own drab existence.

The last two checkpoints were not even manned. I stood in front of an unwatched entry and presently it flew open, and it was Nymphidius Sabinus who emerged. He did not even leer at me, or make comments about getting me alone in a dark room. He merely hissed at me, "Get inside," and shoved me through. The throneroom was full of people and they were all talking at once. I recognized some of them, and none of them looked happy. Seeing me sparked a new round of whispers.

I walked straight into the Empress, who wrapped her arms around me. Her scent overwhelmed me, a heady mélange of perfumes from all the corners of the empire, from musk to civet to attar of roses. She was dressed in the panoply of state, her face white as a toga candida from the lead paint, her lips bright as the lips of a statue of Venus. Her hair was mountainous, and from it peered an ornament studded with rubies that matched her lips.

Everyone at court saw her embrace me, her stola whipping over my face and hiding me from view.

By showing me favour and familiarity, she made the riff-raff look away. I peered through a fold in her stola. At the other end of the room sat Nero, who seemed to almost be swallowed up inside his golden throne. He was not a god at all.

Tigellinus was whispering in his ear and the Emperor pouted, like a child whose toys have been taken away. The tittering in the room was quieting. Himself's face became completely expressionless. Something terrible was about to happen.

The Lady Poppaea Sabina, Goddess, held my fate wrapped in a piece of cloth, it seemed. Idly, she peeled off the fabric so I could look once more at everyone in the hall. The floor was a vast mythological mosaic; she and I were standing right on the head of the heifer Europa, about to be chased by the God. She held my hand and said softly, "He's aware of you. If you play this right, you'll get through this alive. He's after bigger game than you, pretty thing. I'll get you past this hurdle. I promised Petronius."

In front of the throne stood Seneca and Lucan. The poets, old and young, uncle and nephew, had been roughed up a bit, but they were not in chains or anything. They were looking at the floor. Where they stood, in fact, the mosaic portrait the radiant shower of gold, Jupiter in disguise once more, who was about to descend on the beautiful, imprisoned Danaë and impregnate her with the demigod Perseus. They stood, in fact, in a carpet of gold in a blue ocean, on which the chest containing poor Danaë floated. In most of these myths, Jupiter rapes someone, disguised as something.

***

You're going to be raped by Pluto, instead, though.

Just my luck.

Sorry to interrupt. Go on.

***

Finally, after listening to more of Tigellinus's whisperings, Himself the Divinity exploded. "Why?" he screamed.

The poets shrank back as though he had struck them.

"Why? I did nothing but seek your approbation, your acceptance. Yet you conspired to unseat me! Am I Saturn, swallowing his own children, that you must crawl from my guts and kick me off my throne? What did I ever do to you?"

"Divinitas!" they both mumbled, and prostrated themselves.

"What I simply don't understand," said Himself, "is why you haven't both committed suicide yet."

"We'll take care of it immediately, Divinitas."

"Well, don't make me have to kill you. It will be a lot less pleasant. Though undoubtedly fun. For the whole family. Tigellinus, when are the next games?"

"A month, Divinity."

"So they'll have a whole month to stew about whether their property will be forfeited to the state, a whole month to do the right thing so their descendants can still inherit? Where's the drama in a month of reflection? Did Paris have a month to pick which goddess was the most beautiful? Of course not, or there's be no Trojan War, no Homer, no Aeneas fleeing across the Mare Nostrum, no Nero's song soaring over the flames of the second Troy ...."

"How dark the world would be without Nero's song." Poppaea chimed in.

"Where's Petronius? He's the only one I care about. I told Tigellinus that if he was caught in his net, he could throw him back in the river."

"My dear," said Poppaea Sabina, "my poor, dear, beautiful, wounded husband. I have someone here with news of Petronius."

She pushed me forward, into the radius of Divinity. And this is the curious thing: when I stepped into that circle, the buzz of conversation around us seemed to fade to nothing. It was as I was alone there with him, alone in this most public of venues, under the eyes of everyone who was anyone in Rome.

I stood there, eyes downcast, more boy than man. A boy who is a citizen of Rome may set aside the toga praetexta at sixteen, and don the toga virilis of adulthood. I, who had been carried across the sea as a child, I had no age at all, I had no birthday, I had no way to count the passing of time; I was the mirror of my master's will, I was whatever age he saw, and whatever gender, yet always the one possessed, never the possessor.

And the man who possessed the whole world was looking at me, doubtless already deciding my identity for me.

"I've seen this one before, several times," he said. "Once he even came to me as the god Hymen."

"And today?" said the Empress.

"Let's look at you. Boy, look into your Emperor's eyes."

"Yes, Divinitas," I said.

And looked God right in the eye.

Nero was a young man. Perhaps his body was a little less firm than when I saw him, perhaps his eyes more lined. But there was still beauty there. Could a God become shopworn? Was his ignominious end already foreshadowed in those eyes? Suddenly his eyes came much closer. His face rammed down onto mine and he extracted a kiss from my lips. I was shocked. "A second Poppaea," he said. Then, looking at his Empress, he added, "Or perhaps it is my wife who is the second."

"This is Sporus," said Poppaea, "the freedman of Petronius; You've seen him before. You've *wanted* him as a gift, but Petronius cheated you by giving the boy his freedom."

"Really! Then I regret sparing Petronius's life. Guards — go to his house and bring back his head."

"Too late, my dear," said the Empress. "He did himself in last night."

"Oh!" said Himself. "What a beautiful man! You know, he *did* love me. Such devotion! Not like these ... pseudo-poets. Gaius Petronius Arbiter was the real thing." Giving me another little cuddle, he said, "And sending me this thing ... *you* with a penis! What could be more perfect?"

"Sporus was not Petronius's to send," said the Empress. "The boy owns himself. And perhaps even a sizeable chunk of his ex-dominus's estate. But Petronius has sent him with a message."

"A last epistle of devotion, no doubt. Let's have it, boy."

He went to his throne. He sat down. The throne room was designed so a shaft of sunlight from on high would illuminate the one who occupied the seat of power. At that moment he became Jupiter Optimus Maximus and all the other gods. The light lit up his features, and the lines that made him more human were all washed away.

There was silence in the room.

Tigellinus said to Himself, "Caesar, what about Lucan and Seneca?"

The Emperor said to the two poets, "Once you've heard the words of the great Gaius Petronius Arbiter, go home and kill yourselves like proper gentlemen."

"We shall, Divinity," Seneca said with remarkable dignity.

I opened the scroll and began: "To the God that all Rome worships, from a humble wordsmith who has now joined the citizens of Avernus, greeting. Inasmuch as you have given all such pleasure and edification, let me dedicate to you these poor verses. As you are Hyperion, and I am merely a faex expelled from your glorious anus, my words shall not shine like yours, but let me at least say a few lines in the vulgar tongue as an encomium to your refulgent radiance...."

It was my patronus at his most acerbic, demolishing the subject even as he flattered him. Then began the poem itself, written, like Vergil, in hexameters, the most epic of poetic forms, but using the plain speech of the street.

Anxious to cast his gaze / On the womb that had made him a monster
Ripping her belly wide / He thrust in his bloodstained fingers;
Searching in vain for the One / Who had fashioned his soul in her image,
Nothing remained there but Flesh / Nothing remained of his Mother.

***

I expected at that very moment to be sliced in two by Tigellinus's gladius. There was a dead silence in the whole. The fact that the Divinitas had killed his own mother was not something ever mentioned in public, let alone to his face. Poppaea looked at me and her expression was rapt, almost adoring. It seemed that I was not just Petronius's messenger, but sent from all of Rome.

Himself the Divine Caesar bore no expression at all. The only thing in the chamber awash in light, he was as motionless as one of the statues of the Gods. My message was far from over; there was much more to come, pages and pagers of murder, mayhem, debauchery, and moral decay. I waited.

"Lovely, dear boy," said the Divine Nero Claudius Caesar Augustus Germanicus, in a voice utterly devoid of feeling. "Go on, will you? I'm anxious to hear the next bit."

II

APPEASING THE GOD

I admit, my voice was quaking.

As if matricide wasn't bad enough, the catalogue of crimes continued. My recitation went on and on, and as it did, soldiers came and stood behind me in a half-circle, swords drawn, yet Himself the Divinity did not give any signal.

There was Octavia, his first wife:

Slicing the Head off one Wife / and presenting that Head to Another...

There were assorted other gruesome killings, including his treatment of that weird cult from the east:

Setting the City on Fire / and setting on Fire the Guiltless

But my former dominus had saved the worst barbs for

last:

Water quenched not the flames / nor the frenzied screams of the dying;
Setting more fires to contain / the unstoppable blaze was quite useless;
Great Caesar vanquished the flames / with his lyre and his lyrical singing;
Orpheus tamed monsters with melos / Nero slew fire with boredom!

I was doomed as surely as I was standing there. For though some might say the DIvinity's poetry was not the equal of Homer, only Petronius had dared to call it boring. No punishment could be horrific enough for such a crime.

I was as dead as the silence in the chamber.

All eyes were on Himself, Emperor and God. No one looked at me; I was already yesterday's news.

Incredibly, after an unbearably long pause, Nero started to applaud. And laugh. The others in the court were confused, and still didn't say anything. The Emperor cleared his throat. Silence fell again.

"You're all such idiots," he said, "to take this satire at face value. Literal-mindedness is hardly the way to perceive the complexities of the mind of Petronius, creator of *Satyricon!* This child has used his lips to spin filth into gold … the innocence of his utterance shows it. Petronius put such a blasphemous diatribe in the mouth of such a delectable creature in order to tell me that no matter what the critics may say, my work still partakes of the nature of divine, ineffable beauty. Who among you had the breeding, the good manners, to commit suicide even before

I commanded it? He was a friend. I loved him. You other poets are of negligible interest to history."

"In any case, Divinitas," Tigellinus said, "they are traitors. They joined with Calpurnius Piso to attempt to overthrow you."

"Oh, what does that matter?" said Nero. "They've committed a far worse sin than that — writing bad poetry."

The two poets threw themselves on the floor, clasping the hem of his robe.

"Oh, go on," said the Emperor. "Go home and kill yourselves already."

"And the other conspirators, Divinitas?" Tigellinus said.

"Yes, yes, yes." Louder, he announced, "You can all go and kill yourselves now. I mean the conspirators, of course. Everyone else, just carry on. Oh! If any of you conspirators have really *big* estates, I'll seize them, so I'd rather you *not* kill yourself."

"Divinitas," Tigellinus said, "It doesn't really matter. If you want their estates, we can always announce that they didn't commit suicide. Who would know? And even if they did, who would *dare* to know?"

"Are you implying that I, a God, might be in the business of deception?" said Nero.

"I—"

"Quite so," said the Emperor. "For my brother, Jove, is the biggest liar of them all." And he laughed uproariously; and everyone in the room did too, even, I noticed, those who had probably been condemned to death. But Seneca left the room sobbing, supported by Lucan. Presently other people began to leave too, some on their own, others dragged out by soldiers.

I had arrived in the middle of a bloodbath, even though

it was being conducted with terrifying civility. That was the Roman way, though. No one meets their doom with as much sang-froid as a Roman aristocrat.

The throneroom had cleared somewhat. Some slaves and soldiers remained.

"Don't think for a moment," Poppaea whispered in my ear, "that my husband meant a word he said. He knows everything in your message is true. He's always suspected that Petronius didn't like his poetry."

"Am I still going to be killed?" I said softly.

"That depends on you," said the Lady Poppaea. "You've insulted him, and now you must appease him."

"Shall we eat?" said the Divine Nero. "I've had nothing all day."

***

It was about the eighth hour, still mid-afternoon, but we were ushered into a garden where a there was a table laden with what was, I suppose, a light repast by imperial standards. Much of the fare was relatively simple: bread, olives, grapes, figs, wine and salt, but in the center was a platter of peacocks' brains in a honey sauce.

The couch Himself sat in was double-width, and padded enough for a strenuous bout of lovemaking. The Empress and I shared the left couch of this outer triclinium, while on the right sat Tigellinus. At a slight distance sat a secretary, who was reading names from a tablet to Tigellinus, who was passing them on to the Emperor.

The Divine Nero sometimes shook his head, sometimes nodded; the secretary made notes.

"It's a tiring day," said Himself, "when you have to order

a hundred executions before breakfast."

"I'm sorry Calpurnius Piso has put you in such a foul mood, Divinitas," said Tigellinus. "But I think this list just about covers everyone in the plot."

"But the poets — why the poets?"

"You poor thing," Poppaea said to me. "You stumbled into a monstrous conspiracy. Half the senate was plotting deicide."

"Petronius, Petronius," said Nero. "How he loved me. That final satire — so trenchant, so scintillating."

"He loved you?" said Tigellinus. "The man tore you to shreds."

"How little you understand the complexities of artistic expression," said Himself. "You're such a boor, such a brute."

"I know an insult when I hear one."

"I should have you flogged for betraying such a paucity of culture," the Emperor said.

"Then who," said Tigellinus, "would protect you from all those conspirators? Who, as I have demonstrated I think, are lurking behind every bush, every drape, every column."

"Oh, go away, Tigellinus," said the Emperor. "You, too, Epaphroditus. Just leave the list. I'll draw a line through the ones who we've dealt with."

The little clerk, or secretary, slunk away, but not before giving me a look as though he were already plotting my death. Then Tigellinus rose and he too looked at me, but more as a cat regards a mouse.

"Oh, good," said the Lady Poppaea. "We're just family now." She clapped her hands, and a tall, oiled Nubian brought in Hercules on a golden chain. "Hercules misses you, Sporus," she said. "He trusts you. Don't worry. We never eat our friends."

The cheetah meekly crouched at our feet, purring a little.

"Until they're not," said Nero.

The Lady Poppaea said to me, "This is your chance, my little twin brother. The gods, or the gutter? It's your choice. Appease him."

"I don't know how," I said.

"Your master knew how. He appeased him until he couldn't stomach it any more."

The Emperor beckoned to us both with a crook of the finger. The Lady Poppaea and I sat on either side, and Hercules moved as well. I saw that the cheetah unnerved him more than he did me. "It's good to have a spare Poppaea," he said.

"You don't own him," Poppaea said.

"I own everything," he said, a waved to a slave to bring the peacocks' brains. "I do so love peacocks' brains," he said. "Squishy, soft, and succulent." He took one between thumb and forefinger. "Say *ah,*" he said to me, and popped it in my mouth. "Why, look at him swallow!" he said to the Empress. "Can you read and write?" he said to me.

"I'm getting better, Divinitas."

"Fetch the tablet and read me the names. From the top."

"Uh … Plautius Lateranus … Afranius Quintianus … Novius Priscus …"

"You make these names sound so melodious. I love the way you said 'Priscus' … ha, ha, Priskie-Whiskie! Adorable! Just for that, I think I'll let him go."

Poppaea said, "What, just like that?" She sipped at a bowl of wine. "He plotted to have you murdered!"

"A god should be capricious," I said. "Otherwise, he'd

be too predictable, and the gods shouldn't be predictable. Vengeance and clemency should be wielded with apparent randomness."

"You *have* learned something from Petronius," Nero said, laughing. "Well, I was getting tired of my secretary, Epaphroditus. Tired of looking at him. He's starting to age, too. I don't like old people."

"I suppose you wouldn't, Divinity, since you belong with the immortals."

Poppaea reached over and slapped my wrist, giggling.

"Say 'Priscus' again," said Himself. "I love your accent. It's Scythian, is it? Or even further afield?"

"Priscus! Priscus!" I said. And I laughed along with the Emperor.

But deep inside myself, there was a dark place. In that place dwelt my master, dead at his own because of the Emperor's whim. There were other ghosts, too. Hyacinth. And my own childhood, murdered by a pirate rapist. I had not seen my tutor, Aristarchos, since moving to Petronius's house. I longed for the woman named Spider, who for a time had been almost like a mother to me. It occurred to me that perhaps if I managed to get a real position in the imperial hierarchy, I could search for her. I could get things that I wanted, including an identity that was not created by an owner.

Though I had been free for some time now, it took my dominus's death to make me understand.

"Have another brain," said the Emperor, feeding me Himself.

"Divinitas," I said, "how many peacocks does it take to make such a platter?"

"Wonderful!" said Himself. "Poppaea never takes an

interest in how the world runs. For her, the brains just appear by magic. The answer to question is — why — we have our own, private little — to coin a word — *pavonarium*. Would you like to see peacocks — a veritable ocean of peacocks — more bird-brains than even in the Senate?" He clapped hands, dropping a brain onto the grass, though Hercules quickly disposed of it. "Come!"

He took me by the hand and started to pull me in toward the far side of the garden, where there was a fountain cunningly designed like a pair of dolphins. I turned to look at the Lady Poppaea, terrified that I would soon be alone with the God.

"This could be your fortune," she said to me. "You've insulted, you've appeased. Now, Sporus, you must seduce."

III

SEDUCING THE GOD

Alone with the God.

Well … as alone as was humanly possible, as there were plenty of slaves and guards skulking just out of sight, ready to pounce if their God needed rescuing. The Emperor took me by the hand, and we were almost like two schoolboys, except that one held the power of life and death over the other.

"I love peacocks almost as much as Greek tragedy," said Himself.

The cacophony assailed us before we turned a corner and we were in another cloistered walk that surrounded an atrium, but this square was jammed with peacocks. The honking was hideous, and a rancid stench of bird shit fouled the air. A low wooden railing prevented the birds from escaping into the colonnade.

The Divinity pulled out a clear, green disk with a thin gold bezel and began looking at the creatures through it.

He handed me another, a red one. "Looking at the world through an emerald or a ruby," he said, "can sometimes make things ever so much more clear."

I saw the world tinted in rose. It was pretty.

"They are just like the senate," said the Emperor, giggling as he put away his jewel spyglasses. "Endlessly preening and fanning their gaudy feathers, fighting over the peahens, thinking of nothing but their own cocks and bellies! Look there!"

Two of the gaudiest specimens were battling it out at the edge, squawking and flinging each other against the railings. "The green one comes from India, the one with the truly resplendent tail comes from even farther away. And look over there — there's a white one. They are like you, all of them, they come from beyond the empire's edge. And I can have any one of them for breakfast. Just as I can have you for breakfast, Poppaea."

I was going to say, *I'm not Poppaea,* but a little warning went off in the back of my mind. *I'm a freedman,* I told himself, but *but this man owns freedom itself.*

So I just said, "Yes, Divinity," and smiled sweetly.

Himself the Divine Nero took me in his arms, and kissed me, very gently pushing me backwards. To my surprise, a couch broke my fall. Slaves had moved it silently into the colonnade. On either end, a kneeling slave held up a cup of water. I felt my clothes sliding off my back, and glancing warily to one side saw a boy folding them neatly and placing them on a silver tray. The Divinity's robes vanished with equal swiftness, though his were a lot more elaborate than mine, and *his* tray was gold.

Only a few hours had passed since I left my dead patronus's house. I was still alive, and though I had thought my life was over along with Petronius's, I was beginning to think I might survive the night.

And if the price of survival was a sore anus?

I needed to think quickly. My mind was in chaos, still trying to make sense of my grief at losing everything I had only just learned to love. My buttocks collided with the soft cushions in the exact second that my last shred of clothing was removed. Even my *subligaculum* had been untied so deftly I had not noticed until it was gone.

An image entered my consciousness … the first time I saw the Divinity, grunting beneath the thrusts of another freedman, Pythagoras. A Roman man may take the active role in copulating with anything, human or animal, but to receive, to be a *pathicus,* is lower than the lowest. But the Divinity wasn't a Roman *man,* was he? He was a God. The only God who mattered in the real world.

The God who was lowering himself into position, as another slave lifted my legs to afford him access, whose tongue was licking off the last fragments of peacock's brain from my teeth. His paused in mid-kiss and I took advantage to speak. "Divinitas," I said. "I am yours and you may possess me at any time … and yet … I have this secret fantasy … I hardly dare whisper it …"

He looked into my eyes.

"What is it, dearest Poppaea?" he said. "I can fulfill any desire; you must know that."

"Could I … my Lord … could I perhaps possess *you?"*

Nero Claudius Caesar Augustus Germanicus sat bolt upright for a moment. "That is the most impertinent thing I've ever heard." That was it. I was doomed. How could I have been so reckless? I closed my eyes. "Let me get rid of the slaves, first," the Emperor said. "All of you — one hundred paces — and avert your eyes until I command it!" I felt myself being moved into another position and when I opened my eyes, the entire entourage had magically vanished. I knew they must be there, behind columns or furniture. The caterwauling of the peafowl continued, even more strident than before.

I wondered why he had to dismiss all the slaves. The last time I had seen him in such a position, it had been at a wild dinner party with dozens of onlookers from Rome's highest echelons. But as I was to find out, there were as many Neros as there are hours in a year.

The Emperor smiled. "I know that you're not actually Poppaea," he said softly.

Nero reclined with his face turned up towards me, his haunches raised. I knew what I must do. I thought of my burning village, of the vicious pirate slavemonger who "broke me in." I thought of my master, Petronius, who had never once forced me at all. I thought of Hyacinth, and of Hylas, still waiting for at Petronius's villa, probably unsure of whether he would ever see me again.

And I thought of the first time I had heard Nero sing. He did have a certain art, he did have some vision of something beautiful, though his muse might have been twisted and depraved. I thought of how I'd fallen in love at first sight, and how quickly I had been disillusioned. And when I looked at Himself, master of the world, I also saw a small boy inside, an unloved boy, a boy who recognized flattery yet had come to believe it was proof of love. And in the moment, I did not fear him.

"Divinitas!" I whispered.

In so small a voice that he barely be heard above the squawking of the peacocks, he said, "Call me Lucius."

By time I emerged from the encounter, I had acquired a ruby lens for myself, along with a small pouch of aurei. Himself did not command me to stay, but told me to go home and take care of my affairs.

"That was an exhausting bout," he said, "and I shall write an ode about it. Perhaps, I shall rhapsodize about the young Troilus, receiving the heroic member of Achilles. As a poet, I must experience all things, as you know. We shall consider our little tryst ... artistic research."

"And Petronius's letter, Divinity? Shall I burn it?"

"Not at all. I shall keep it. I may need an excuse, one day, to have you executed."

"Yes ... Lucius."

He slapped my face. "Never in public!" he whispered harshly. So saying, he left for an inner room, and left the slaves to escort me to back to the palace entrance.

I was standing in the hallway, rubbing my cheek. It seemed that Marcus and some other soldiers had been waiting to take me make, and that Petronius's litterbearers were standing by beyond the entrance. Dully I made my way toward the door.

But as the slaves opened the portal, the Lady Poppaea came upon me as though by accident — I knew of course that she never did anything by accident —and pretended to be surprised at seeing me.

"Oh!" she said. "You're alive."

"I think so."

A slave behind her was carrying a bowl of snow, perhaps meant for cooling a drink; Poppaea dipped her hands in the snow and patted my cheek. "He does like it rough sometimes," she said with a wink. "And yet, in a few hours, you have managed to insult, appease, *and* seduce him. You're doing better even than me."

Without warning, appallingly, I started to cry. I was nobody. I had no real home, no parents, no patron ... and I was in a lion's den. Roman men do not cry. I was neither Roman, not a man.

"So," said the Lady Poppaea, "your poised exterior does have a cracking point." But she was not being cruel, just truthful.

"I'm just a child!" I said.

The mistress of the world took me in her arms. I held her tight — too tight — as though she were my mother. She wiped my tears with a fold of her stola. "There, there," she said softly. "It will be good to have you here now and then. I don't know what your status will be, as you are a freedman and I don't know whether Petronius has left you anything — or indeed whether the Divinitas will contravene the custom by seizing Petronius's property — but I am going to need relief."

"Relief?"

"Yes, Sporus," said the Lady Poppaea Sabina. "I am pregnant."

IV

DOMINUS

The Lady Poppaea Sabina, Empress of the World, had not yet told the Divinitas.

"I don't know," she said, "if he actually ripped open his mother's womb, as the rumors contend. But I think I'll protect mine, at least until it shows."

She handed me a second pouch of gold before I left. It was not yet sunset, but though I had left with nothing but a damning letter, I was returning with 40 aurei and a giant ruby. Enough to hire a legionary for three years.

"A few more visits to the palace and you could have a private army," said Marcus as he helped me into the litter. I was woozy; after an hour's exercise with the Divinitas I had downed several cups of snow-cooled Lesbian wine.

***

When I reentered the house of my former master, there was something of a reception committee, although all wore the dark clothes of mourning and many had ripped their clothes and lacerated their cheeks. I could hear female slaves wailing from inner room. Petronius had been moved to a taller bier beneath the masks of his ancestors and the household gods. A libitinarius was still watching over the body and arranging and rearranging the folds of his cloak. The house was dark.

Yet Hylas broke away from the group and embraced me before remembering his place and, kneeling, removed my caligae, whispering *"Salve, domine."* He waved away the foot-washer slave, took the jar and washed my feet himself.

"No need to call me your dominus," I said. "Not after all we went through together."

But Croesus said, "The boy knows his place."

Hylas went inside to fetch me a toga pulla so I would look less festive, and he draped it over my tunica.

"Dark becomes you," said Marcus Vinicius as he looked on approvingly.

Then Croesus said, "If I ever whipped you, Sporus, be assured I was only doing my job, and I drove the lash as lightly as I dared." He looked at me strangely. Had things changed so much?

"Never left a mark," I said, laughing, "though you really made it sting."

"It's an art," he said, "hurting the slaves without damaging them."

"You are never to beat Hylas," I said.

"That is entirely your decision, Gaius Petronius Sporus," said Croesus, who had not addressed me so while his master was living.

"If Sporus want," Hylas said, "Sporus beat me himself."

And he suddenly started crying. "Me think you no come back."

"You," I said, "are going to stop speaking Latin in that barbarous fashion. I've been here less time than you, and I know a nominative from an accusative." To Marcus I said, "Can I get Aristarchos to tutor him?"

"I doubt he's for sale," Marcus said, "but we can go to the market on the Kalends and buy him a good tutor. It will be more than 4,000 sesterces, mind you. That's all the money you have. But don't worry, I'll buy him for you as a … wedding gift."

"Wedding? We only *did* it once."

Everyone laughed, breaking the pall. I was embarrassed, I could feel my cheeks reddening. I realized that they all *knew*. My trip to the palace only had two possible outcomes, the other one being me nailed to a cross somewhere. It was secretly a bit delicious to realize, on the other hand, that none of them would probably have imagined that in the second outcome, it would be *I* who would end up doing the nailing.

Croesus said, "We've made up the master's cubiculum for you. He would have wanted that." So I would sleep in the bed Petronius died in. I felt a twinge of panic.

"Shouldn't *Marcus* have the master's quarters?"

"I have my own house, my own servants," said Marcus Vinicius. "I'll be the master here in name; Croesus will keep up this place for me and answer to me directly; I'll take some of the slaves that were Petronius didn't set free, but you'll have a small household at your disposal and you will be my deputy. As for money, you'll get a small allowance from out estates in the country. Not much. You could start a business: no shame in that, you're not of noble blood."

"I don't know anything about business," I said.

"Buying and selling delicati?" Croesus said. "Obviously you would have insider knowledge, and a good eye."

"Croesus," Marcus said, "I don't think he wants to put anyone through what he went through."

"If not prostitution, what else could you profit from?" said Croesus.

"I want to know more about poetry," I said, "and music."

"A gentleman of leisure, then," Croesus said, without a trace of irony.

Marcus said, "I'll have to buy the young dominus a more expensive tutor, then." He started to leave; as a Roman officer, he probably had something to do other than hold a frightened boy's hand; I could understand that.

And yet, my terror overcame me. I did not want to lie down on that bed, not by myself, not even with Hylas. I wanted someone to comfort me, someone stronger than me. I reached out to Vinicnius with the only means of persuasion I knew. "Marcus!" I cried out. "Marcus, sleep with me!"

He understood, and stayed.

***

Though not in my bed. He *really* understood, you see.

He sat on a sella beside my couch. At my feet, curled tight, like a cat, was Hylas, who was fast asleep. Slaves fall asleep quickly; it's the only time they achieve freedom.

I just lay there for a long time, sobbing into the cushions, while Vinicius stroked my hair. After a great deal of time had passed, and the oil in the lamp had been twice refilled, my weeping subsided a little and I finally felt brave enough to ask him what today was all about.

"Gaius Calpurnius Piso," Marcus said with a sigh.

"Who's that? Another bad poet?"

"Worse. A conspirator. I have forty-nine more people on the arrest list tomorrow … and later I have to speak the eulogium for your patronus."

The lamp flickered. His face, lined with concerned, looked at me out of a pool of shadow. "You have to kill forty-nine people tomorrow?"

"Not in person, no, but if I don't, I'll have to send someone. Tigellinus has the master list. You'd recognize most of the names."

***

"A conspiracy is like a plague. You breathe it, you catch it, you die. Was my uncle Petronius evil? You know he was not. Were Lucan and Seneca evil? Plots within plots. They planned to kill Nero and make Piso Emperor, but inside that plot was a plot to kill Piso and make Seneca Emperor, so that the conspirators wouldn't appear self-serving."

"Did Seneca even know?"

"It doesn't matter. He breathed it. He caught it. He's dead, or as good as dead. When this is over, half the noble families in Rome will be gone, and Himself will be much, much richer. He might even be able to afford to finish his Golden House."

But I was thinking that my patronus would be laid on a funeral pyre tomorrow, and that Marcus would try to offer words of praise and comfort, but that I would not be comforted. "What will you say in your eulogium?" I said, feeling tired now, though I was afraid to feel asleep with my patronus's shade perhaps hovering over me.

"What I say will be forgotten in minutes," said Marcus Vinicius, "seeing that Himself is going to be speaking as well. He wouldn't miss the opportunity to perform a new ode. And you know that tragic odes are his speciality."

"The Divinity will perform a eulogy … over someone whose death he is responsible for?"

"He doesn't think of it that way. He thinks Petronius did it out of devotion. Even your little reading, a last taste of his satyrical wit. Petronius was always the only person who dared to criticise Himself. Even though Tigellinus got him on the death list, I think Nero meant to find a way around it. You loved my uncle. In his way, Himself too loved Petronius."

As I finally drifted into fitful sleep, I was thinking: *for the Gods, there is no difference between love and death.*

V

FUNERAL

And then came the funeral of my patronus. What can I say? The tiresome, fully paid-for wailing of professional mourners first. A Greek theme predominated, as befit Petronius's literary stature, meaning hired women beating their breasts and the keening of double flutes, doleful but tinged with eroticism. I was an insignificant little one in this throng of important persons. They included such senators as had not already been arrested or gone off to commit suicide.

***

The master of the world had no peer, and certainly master in poesy, either, not any more. Homer was long gone; Ovid had been dead, in exile, for half a century; Virgil, too had been gone as long. Horace, too. The three legends; long gone before my birth.

And the legends of our own time? Petronius was gone too, now. His passion, his love for beautiful things, his brutal wit, all gone. Until then, he was the only Roman I could sleep with and feel safe. I did not know if I would ever find another.

Seneca and Lucan had already vanished. Whether they had committed suicide, I did not know.

The funeral procession went from my patronus's domus all the way down to the forum; Petronius was important enough to merit a public eulogy, and his suicide had rendered his death entirely honorable, no matter what acts of insurrection he might have been accused of. The assemblage of priests, acolytes, mourners and instrumentalists clogged up the street and occasionally zigzagged to avoid a pile of dung. By now I was more used to riding in a litter, shielded by a curtain from the cacophony of scents: perfume, shit, baking bread and roasting meat and urine being delivered to laundries. As I walked, Rome clung to my nostrils, mixed into my sweat.

It was a long day, beginning at the eighth hour, the afternoon sun still cruel.

First, the forum, and Marcus Vinicius's was but one of a number of "warm-up" eulogies, for it was said that Himself planned to deliver the climactic words. Marcus spoke of his uncle's many kindnesses, his discriminating aestheticism, even of me. But no one looked my way; I was a boy in a toga pulla, indistinguishable from any other mourner. The kohl around my eyes was smudged from tears. Hylas stood behind me, staring at the ground. I was nowhere near the great senators and patricians. I was with Croesus and the other ex-slaves, crowded toward the back, in the shadow of an archway.

At length came Himself, preceded by a honour guard of Praetorians, to the raucous bellow of bucinae and cornua.

Behind them came women dressed as maenads, each beating a tympanon or shaking a sistrum. Above the racket was the shrieking of the double aulos players, like a tempest in the trees. The music was bloodcurdling, as though the gates of Hades were screeching open.

And abruptly, it stopped.

A burst of chatter followed, became still.

I heard Tigellinus barking out a command.

The double line of guards and musicians separated into walls of an alley; Himself was arriving, carried in a litter by sixteen matched, oiled Nubians, each wearing only a white loincloth. The musk of mingled man-sweat and olive oil wafted towards us.

Behind him came the litter of the Empress, borne by sixteen perfectly matched blonde women, pale, wearing only a black subligaculum; the perfect contrast to the Divinity's litter, black on white, white on black.

In the quiet, the Emperor tuned his kithara.

He approached the rostrum that overlooked the bier.

As one who had once served as a *consul suffectus,* Petronius was entitled to wear the toga picta, though I had never seen him dressed that way. In his hands he held the shards of the wine-dipper that he knew the Divinitas coveted. The Emperor would have to look at this smashed work of art during his eulogy; Petronius was having yet another last laugh.

The Lady Poppaea Sabina had a sharp eye. She saw me right away, even though I was trying to hide behind my patronus's steward. She crooked a finger. I stepped forward hesitantly, but, heedless of decorum, she swooped toward the crowd as the guards hastened to protect her, and pulled me out.

"Look what I've found, Lucius!" she said to the Emperor. Several people nearby, hearing her, were shocked at her disrespect for the God, though she herself was technically divine.

"Petronius's Giton," he said. "And *your* replacement, should anything ever befall you."

As if anything could befall the mistress of the world, who held everything in the palm of her hand.

Himself bade me approach. I looked back. I could see the apprehension in Hylas's eyes. I walked cautiously towards him.

"Come closer," he said. "I want to see what inspired Petronius."

I went right up to him. Of course, I was afraid, even though only a few days ago I had been ramming my small manhood into the sacred shit-hole. I tried to overcome my stark terror by imagining Himself squirming on the couch, the slaves all tastefully out of sight or averting their eyes, amid the squawking of peacocks.

The Emperor placed me on his left, and Poppaea stood on his right. He looked from me to her. "I don't know which Muse is the more beautiful," he said softly. "It's a pity Petronius killed himself; I can't legally seize his property now."

"He's free," Poppaea reminded him. "You couldn't have seized him anyway."

"My secretary, Epaphroditus, whom you met," said Himself to me, "himself has a slave named Epictetus, who is a great philosopher, though no older than you, Sporus. And you know what this boy said to me? 'No man is free, save he be master of himself.'"

I remembered Ephaphroditus, the little clerk who wrote

down the names of everyone who should be executed.

"I freed Epaphroditus, you know," Himself said. "He was so helpful in choosing who I needed to get rid of after that conspiracy."

He looked at me again. Perhaps he too was reliving our little tryst among the peacocks. He smiled a little, and I smiled too. Then he said, "Perhaps he should have saved the wine dipper, and smashed you instead. Sporus in one piece rebukes me more than a voiceless piece of ancient crockery."

I recoiled a little, in fear, but he said, "If you're going to survive the palace, my child, you'd best learn to tell when I'm joking."

"The palace, Divinity?" I said.

"Yes. You're moving in."

Poppaea clapped her hands. "Thank you, my Lord!" she said. "Two of me will be able to divide the work."

"One to bear the next Divinitas, the other to fuck," said the Emperor.

He stepped toward the rostrum. Silence fell again. But in the distance there were still murmurs of the city, for Rome never sleeps. Now I recognized more of the courtiers. There was Epaphroditus, busy with a wax tablet, a boy in tow — not a delicatus to be sure, as he was decidedly plain — but so seriously-looking that he had a kind of charisma.

Was that the philosopher slave?

I saw Tigellinus, and Nymphidius, too, especially since he was leering at me. Then he sort of swivelled and leered at Hylas, whom I had left behind in the crowd. He even leered at a slave of Epaphroditus. He was omnivorous in his leering.

Marcus Vinicius was in a group of aristocrats, distinguishable by his toga pulla. As a relative — and heir — he was most clearly in morning, with his ripped garment of dark wool, like mine. But most of them had not bothered to dress appropriately; they were more festive, with a riot of colour, some even in silk. Most had come for the Emperor's recital, not to pay their respects to Petronius. Indeed, they had probably been "invited" and needed to show their faces, to prove they had not participated in the Pisonian conpiracy.

The proof might not have been quite enough for some; as the Emperor's recital began, I could see Tigellinus putting some of the guests under arrest and they were being marched away.

The Divinity began. He struck a few deep tones on his instrument. A tympanum thudded and a cymbalum tinkled. The Emperor sang a long, modulated melisma of anguish:

Ah, ah, ah, pheu, pheu!
Seven were my daughters,
seven are their corpses,
pierced with arrows
strewn over the bodies
of my seven sons…

"Not Niobe again!" Poppaea whispered to me, alluding to one of the gems of Nero's repertoire, the the virtuosic — and endless — *Niobe weeping for her children.* "It'll be the ninth hour before it's over."

VI

LUCIUS DOMITIUS PARIS

As the Divinitas continued his dirge, his public tensed. It would not do to leave, or even to nod off, lest one be noticed. In fact, some of the centurions were watching the audience quite carefully. Woe to anyone who needed to relieve himself!

I listened. Nero's voice was beautiful — I knew that already. Each pitch was carefully placed, and the melismatic ornaments shaped with such smoothness that they wuthered like a mountain wind in the moonlight.

His portrayal of Niobe's grief had real conviction, nobility even. But Niobe had seven sons and seven daughters, each shot dead by a dart from the bow of the God of the Sun.

Her grief would be a rich meal of many courses, each more lugubrious than the last.

He was just on the first of the fourteen children, but he was already drawn deep into himself, drawing on the passion of his inner daemons. The audience became a little less tense, for when the Divinitas was like this, he rarely saw anyone else, so fixed was his gaze on high Olympus.

Of course, the Praetorians' scrutiny was still on the audience, so they could not misbehave that much.

Then, as the Emperor continued his song, someone stepped out of the crowd.

Man or woman, it was hard to tell. He wore a tunica that went past his knees, dyed in imperial purple with gold embroidery. And he began to move, in a sinuous dancelike improvisation, in front of the Divinity's field of vision, his every gesture eerily synchronizing with the Emperor's song.

Each sweeping hand movement amplified Nero's tears. Leaping and crouching, the mime portrayed Niobe's inner rage behind the outward lamentation.

I heard the Lady Poppaea Sabina whisper: "Lucius Domitius Paris."

I whispered back … "Not Lucius Domitius!" For that was the Emperor's real name, in the obscure time before his uncle Claudius adopted him and made him heir to the Empire.

"No. A freedman of the Divinitas's adoptive grandmother-in-law, hence the name. As a slave, he was called Paris. He's the most famous actor in Rome."

"But … upstaging the Divinitas!"

"Delicious! And there's nothing the Emperor can do; he'd have to break off his song."

As the Emperor's song increased in intensity, so did the mime's performance. When Nero sang a high note that never seemed to end, so Paris seemed to hang in the empty air, defying the pull of the earth. When the Emperor sang rapid scales, Paris flew like the wind. When the the Divinitas sang twisted ornaments, Paris twisted his body into the shapes of the music.

By the time Nero's song ended, all eyes were on the dancer.

The Divinitas ended with a cadential flourish, striking the strings of the *kithara* and letting out a howl of anguish as Niobe's grief finally transcended words. The mime whirled and whirled until he was a blur, then sank down before the Emperor's feet, his lips landing right on the feet of the God.

Applause rang out. And I knew it was not for the Emperor. I feared for the man's life, especially when Tigellinus thrust himself out of the throng and a brace of Praetorians dragged him to his feet.

"This man conspired with the Pisonians," Tigellinus said. "Shall we execute him on the spot, or allow him one last performance at the circus?"

"Easy, Tigellinus," said Nero. "We're at a funeral, and you heard all the applause."

"I was a mere appendage to your performance, Divinitas," said Paris, brazenly insincere it seemed to me, "helping to amplify your words so they would reach out beyond the limited acoustics of this forum."

"You see, Tigellinus? Don't be such a boor."

"You can't be too tough on traitors," Tigellinus said, sulking. There was something unspoken going on between the master of the world and his right hand man. Some kind of power play. In that moment, I knew that Tigellinus despised the Emperor.

But Nero did not see it.

Paris's toadying, too, was dripping with irony. I could see it. I was bristling on my Emperor's behalf, almost certain that Nero might order him beheaded right in front of the crowd. But the Emperor did not see it.

The applause continued, crescendoed even — the crowd did not seem to realize that Paris was in danger of being instantly executed, rather they seemed to think the guards were flanking him because the Emperor was about to bestow some signal honour upon him.

The Divinitas held up his hand for silence.

"Well done, Lucius Domitius Paris," he said. "Your eloquence has earned you pardon."

'Forgive me, Divinitas," said Paris. "I am an artist, easily tricked by politicians."

"I know," said Nero. "It happens to me all the time."

The Divinitas was biding his time. Now, I understand. He was saving Paris, the way one might keep a juicy morsel on the plate to savour later, like an unborn dormouse dipped in honey.

"You will come to me at the palace," the Emperor said, "and you'll teach me all your secrets. I labour so much at my music, yet you reach the zenith of your art without producing a single sound. I shall learn from you."

"I dare not instruct a God," said Paris.

"Really!" said Nero. "But I am a good and gracious God. Compliant. Docile, even. And ever so humble. I have not an iota of hubris."

"Of course not, Divinitas."

I was starting to sense more clearly what life with Himself the Divinity might be like. Never being sure for a second where you stood. Death lurking treachery behind every turn of phrase, every miscalculated step. Ironies within ironies. And my patronus lived that life. Until it killed him.

Himself seemed bored. I did not think he would want to

follow the procession out beyond the city walls, where the actual cremation would occur. And indeed, he turned, and the entire retinue turned with him, the spokes of a wheel with the Divinitas at its centre.

The Empress whispered to me, "Go burn your master's body and send him to the next life. But soon, he'll send for you. And when he does, you'll go to him. You'll listen. Everyone hears him, but nobody listens. He doesn't know it yet, but he needs you."

How could the Emperor need me?

***

I watched as the litterbearers, soldiers, and all the hangers-on receded into the distance. Our household made a tawdry spectacle by comparison, though Croesus had not skimped. Our procession moved slowly and with the proper solemnity to the closest city gate from the Forum, the Porta Fontinalis; a cremation in the Field of Mars could be considered appropriate for Petronius because of his brief time as a consul, though he was not a military man.

Here, we laid my patronus on a high bier of good wood, accompanied only by the shards of the wine dipper which the Emperor, surely, had not failed to notice in the Forum.

As a nod to tradition, a pair of gladiators fought to the death in front of the pyre. This was a solemn match, the fighters knowing there would be no rescue from the mob if they fought well and lost. They were skilled men, the most expensive that Vinicius could afford, provided by one of the best lanistas in Capua. The battle was protracted; neither was willing to be an easy sacrifice to the spirit of the dead poet.

"This is the real thing," Croesus told me. "The circus is

just entertainment. In ancient times, before even the Republic, prisoners fought to the death to honour a fallen commander. Over the centuries, this noble custom devolved into pygmies fighting amazons and ostrich races."

As his heir, Marcus set the pyre alight.

I told Marcus Vinicius that the Empress had told me I would be summoned soon, that the Divinitas "needed" me.

Marcus said, "I need you too, Sporus."

"Why?"

The flames rose. So did my tears.

"Tigellinus wants the mansion, perhaps the up-country estate as well. And Nymphidius wants *you* as a kind of spoil of war."

"But Petronius committed suicide entirely properly, and his belongings cannot be seized," I said.

"We need you at court," Marcus said. "To *remind* him."

It seemed that everyone needed me there ... and not for any reason that did me any good. At the moment, I longed to be a slave again. When I belonged to Petronius, everything made sense. Now, it was all uncertainty.

***

I thought about slavery again, after the long trudge home. I was in my former master's bath, with a kylix of cold wine, lying in soothing hot water with my feet raised.

Hylas was rubbing my feet. With each squeeze I felt a twinge of pleasure; we had walked, in total, for many miles, then stood for an eternity while the Emperor sang and Paris mimed.

It occurred to me that Hylas's feet probably hurt as much

as mine, yet he wasn't complaining. He worked my feet methodically, his eyes downcast. He was taller than when I first met him. I wondered whether, like Hyacinth, he feared losing his looks.

"Don't you want to be free, Hylas?" I asked him.

"Why?" he said. "Massage no good?"

He applied more pressure to my soles; I think he was worried that by that question, I meant I was not happy with him.

"No, it is fine. But ... your feet are in pain, too. Shall I rub yours?"

"No good. You are dominus."

"I'm no more than a year older than you, Hylas."

"Younger, maybe," he said. "You more beautiful."

I said, "But doesn't it bother you that you have to do whatever I command, no matter when or where?"

"No."

"I mean, I could say to you, 'fellate me this very second,' and even though you're dog-tired, you'd have to do it. Doesn't it bother you?"

"Of course not. Me love you, dominus."

"Domine," I said. "When you're talking to me you have to use the vocative case." For just a second, fear flecked the boy's eyes, as if I was about to order a whipping. I immediately felt like a fool. The comfort of the clouds of steam, condensing on the marble walls, was coming to me because some overworked creature was stoking a furnace in the basement, sweating like a pig. The snow-cooled wine I was sipping at came from someone's labour, and the snow was delivered by a runner from the distant hills. The world runs on slavery, I thought, and I should thank the Gods I am no longer one.

"That's enough," I said. "Help me out and then do the olive oil and the strigil."

The oil was scented and Hylas drove the scraper with a firm hand, making my skin tingling, vibrant. "You almost make me forget," I said, "that I'm holding the future of the Petronius *gens* in my hands, and if I say the wrong thing all these people whom I have come to love will fall into the hands of Tigellinus."

"Me do it now?" said Hylas, eyeing my stiffening member.

I could not help laughing. "The night we met," I said, "you tried to steal my mirror."

"That night you not my dominus. Tonight my life belong you. *Corpus, os, culus.* You take."

His face moved closer to my groin. "Don't be impertinent," I said. He darted back as if I'd slapped him. It pained me that I had fallen so easily into the habit of being a master. Had I forgotten so quickly? So I smiled, trying to signal that he should never be afraid of me.

But later, while I slept, I cannot tell what he did; for in the morning, I woke alone, and I felt more refreshed than I had felt in a long while.

But not for long, for over my simple breakfast of bread and olives, the Praetorians came to escort me once again to the Palatine.

VII

THE BOY PHILOSOPHER

If I had thought that, after being collected from home at the crack of dawn, I would be immediately be ushered into the Emperor's presence, I was wrong. The soldiers had allowed me an attendant, so I took Hylas, letting him walk alongside the litterbearers, and keeping the curtain slightly opened so we could look at each other.

"Did you do something to me last night?" I said.

"No. You must conserve. Emperor will want all."

"But I feel much more calm."

"I hold you through the night. You cry in your sleep."

I had barely wept through my patronus's death. They have taught me that a good Roman boy does not weep, but keeps a serious demeanour. I was glad someone had seen me weep and I was glad it was Hylas. Someone else would use it against me.

Once we arrived at the palace, I was greeted by Epaphroditus, who hustled me off to a little room without windows. Hylas followed, but the Emperor's secretary dismissed the guards who had escorted us.

"Let's find you some quarters," he said.

"Quarters?"

"Well, yes. I can hardly expect the Divinitas's latest plaything to sleep in the hallways."

"I didn't know I was moving in."

"You're not," said the diminutive secretary, "but if Himself were, on a whim, in a strange mood, to *hint* at it, and you did not *already* have your own apartments here, I might get a whipping, you know."

"Not you," I said. "You're more powerful than most senators. Surely you don't get whipped. Why, Himself told me, he personally freed you."

"But he forgets. And sometimes it's not tactful to correct a God."

"Still, I can't believe that you, a learned clerk, someone who knows where the bodies are buried and who's screwing whose wife … would have the indignity of —"

"Not that often," he said, sighing. "The Divinity would have to be pretty drunk. But you'll bear the brunt of that, more often than I will, I dare say."

"The beating?" My heart sank.

"No, no, he doesn't damage pretty things," said Epaphroditus. "I mean the drunken moments. You will see him at his worst, you will see the Himself he doesn't let others see."

"You seem pretty certain of that."

"Whatever. Now, let's find you an appropriate lodging. Not too far from Himself, in case he needs you at some strange hour. He won't come to you; you'll be summoned. It's not that he has a problem with stumbling to your room in a stupor for a quick bout of sex. It's because this palace has too many rooms, and more keep being added, and he loses his way more often that he cares to admit."

***

Now this Epaphroditus had a slave named Epictetus. The slave who was a philosopher. I had seen him lurking around on another occasion, and Himself had actually quoted something he said at the funeral.

It was this boy whom Epaphroditus sent to scout out an apartment for me. He led us down corridors and through subterranean tunnels. Epictetus moved rapidly, like a rodent. The labyrinth was his element. We emerged in a secret garden surrounded by a colonnade; in the garden stood a marble likeness of the Lady Poppaea. When Hylas saw the statue, he gasped.

"Dominus? *Domina?"* he whispered.

I gazed up at the Lady Poppaea. She was painted in vivid, lifelike hues. It was as if she were about to draw breath. She wore a simple stola, white with a little purple, the folds of the fabric so well painted that one could believe they would rustle in the wind. There was a whiff of frankincense; someone had been worshipping her image.

"This is the Empress's own garden," Epictetus said. He looked me over again. "We all know why *you* are here."

"I'm the Empress with a penis," I said ruefully. "A divine gift, and a divine curse."

"If the Emperor finds his way here," Epictetus said, "he'll double his chances of finding his beloved."

I have to say that all this was making me uneasy. It was not really my intention to live at the palace at all. "This is all ... just in case, isn't it?" I asked. "There's no actual command for me to live here. I'm right, aren't I?"

"True," said Epictetus, "but my master has learned to be prepared for anything."

At length, Epictetus picked out something far too lavish. It was roomier than any chamber in Petronius's house. To Hylas's delight, there was a mural that depicted the legend of Hylas and the nymphs, with a frustrated Hercules watching behind some bushes. "It's about me," Hylas said, laughing.

"One slave won't be enough," Epictetus said. "We'll have to buy you a few more. A few to look after your wardrobe, hair and makeup. Someone to run errands. I see you already own a puer delicatus, but he'll be over the hill in a year."

"I can choose a few slaves?"

"Within reason. Unless your requirements are beyond the pale, I am sure it will be covered from the imperial household management funds."

"Can I really buy anyone I want, within reason?" For I was thinking, perhaps I could find Spider, redeem her out of whatever she had been sold into. And then I would know something approaching a mother's affection.

There was a chest with tunicae and two togas, one pure white one and one with the purple stripe of one who has not yet attained manhood. There were also a few women's things, a stola and assorted embroidered cloths for draping.

"We'll bring you more clothes to pick from. And an assortment of jewelry, though I am sure more will be bestowed on you."

"I see."

"Any special requirements? Bathing in asses' milk, pearls dissolved in vinegar, that kind of thing?"

His delivery was so deadpan I did not know if he was being serious.

"People ask for such things?" I said.

"It's said that Cleopatra did, when she was in Rome as a guest of the Divine Julius."

"Who Cleopatra?" said Hylas.

"A Queen who killed herself eighty years ago," Epictetus said, "during the reign of the Divine Augustus."

"Well, but I'm not a Queen, just some kind of amusement."

"There are things in life that you have no control over. But if you *should* become powerful, have courage and use that power to do good."

This boy was special. He had a kind of serenity. He sounded like a much older man.

"I know I do," Epictetus said, reading my mind. "I read a lot. You will always find me in the Imperial library. One day I'll be a philosopher."

"I think you are one already," I said.

"True enough," he said. "I live inside my mind, and so the world matters little. Now, please ..." he gestured. Slaves who had shadowed us, keeping just out of sight, now entered the room. They carried armfuls of clothing, and more clothing in cedarwood chests. "Some of these belonged to ... other lovers," said the boy. "Some are forgotten; for others, it didn't end so well. And here, a stola that used to belong to Actë, who loved Himself before he became a God. That's a rarity from the east, a silk so sheer you can see right through it and it is like wearing nothing at all; it took three years to weave, three more to get to Rome."

More slaves came with more supplies; jugs of wine,

dishes with dates, bread and salt, an amphora of fresh water; cosmetics; trinkets; a miniature shrine with an obscene little Priapus statue, presumably to bless any matings that might ensue.

"I should really ask you if you approve the room," Epictetus said, "but there is really no point. These are the best quarters available. If you need anything, send the boy."

"Send him where?" I said.

"He's a bright lad. He'll find whatever you're looking for. Slaves are good at sniffing things out. You should know, Sporus."

"You no call my master *dominus?*" said Hylas.

I put my hand on his shoulder. "This boy is everyone's equal," I said. I knew that from the way he carried himself. He had not been taught to be servile, nor had he learned it by himself. He was going to be extraordinary. Nero's circle of poets all aspired to be Stoics, but they were not averse to hypocrisy, when expedient. But this boy was the real thing.

"I will leave you now," he said. The other slaves disappeared as if by magic, and all the clothes and trinkets had been carefully put away in chests and baskets. To Hylas, he said, "Have your master dressed and bathed by the eleventh hour; nothing fancy, mind you; I think the Divinitas has an escapade in mind for after cena."

"An escapade?"

"Oh yes," said the boy. "This is Rome — where the night can burn as brightly as the day. Did your former master keep you chained up in the house day and night? Don't tell me you haven't sampled the night life."

VIII

ROMA PER NOCTEM

When the summons came, it was Vinicius.

I was happier to see him than almost anyone. After Epictetus left, I had been sitting in the room, watching Hylas sort through my clothes. I did not feel like a resident of the royal palace, let alone like the "favorite" of a god, as Ganymede was the cup-bearer to Jupiter. I was disoriented. If I left the room and shouted for a slave, would anyone listen?

Was Lady Poppaea's chamber nearby? Were there mistresses and concubines in other apartments, applying makeup and trying on garments, just in case there was visitation from the Divinitas? I sat in my suite alone, well, not if you count Hylas, but he had taken on his new role as my slave, and no longer behaved as though he were my friend.

Vinicius said, "You are overdressed."

I had thought myself elegantly simple, a simple tunica, a stola of unpatterned silk. The slightest dash of kohl and my lips shone with a hidden fire. There was a mirror of polished bronze in the room, so expansive I could see the whole upper half of myself, not like the shard that Hylas had wanted to steal from me once.

"Overdressed?" I said.

"Yes," said Marcus Vinicius. "Take Hylas's clothes. Tonight you will be a scruffy little slave. Hylas, take off the makeup and dirty your dominus's hair a bit."

"Where am I going?"

"Wherever the Divinitas wants," Marcus said. "Leave your slave here. If he gets hungry, I'm sure he can find the kitchens."

"Are you coming?"

Marcus laughed. "I don't move in the same exalted circles as you do. You were my Uncle's Giton. Now you are Jupiter's Ganymede."

It was not a comforting thought. "Your uncle didn't have thunderbolts," I said.

"He *did* have satire."

"And what good did it do him?"

"Petronius will live on, little Giton," said Marcus Vinicius. "Whereas the poetry composed by Himself…."

He did not say more. Who knew who might be listening? But after I changed my clothes a few more times, and looked unremarkable enough to please him, he led me from the room, to a passageway with a secret door, and a stairwell that led downwards. The light was dismal, just a torch here and there. "We're going halfway down the Palatine!" I said. But eventually we arrived at a kind of back entrance, where a litter awaited. It was dark. This was no Imperial palanquin, but a plain transport, the kind of thing a minor official might use. The bearers were Nubians, blending into the night. The turned as one to look at me, their eyes like stars.

Marcus waved me in. "Hurry," he said. "God waits for no one, not even Ganymede." With a great deal of trepidation, I drew the curtain a little way. Someone seized both my arms and dragged me inside, and I was alone with the Divinitas, only for the second time.

An oil lamp with an image of Priapus was the only light. The Divinitas peered at me as though I were some exotic animal. "Sporus?"

"Yes, Divinitas."

He cackled. "You look suitably plebeian," he said. "Do I?"

I must admit that he did not. For though the tunic he wore was unwashed, and his caligae scratched and worn, there was still the perfect hair, and the fragrance he wore. I should have said, "No one would be followed for a minute," but I knew that was not the required answer.

"My Lord," I said, "allow me to muss up your hair a little."

"Ah! The finishing touch! Perceptive of you."

I ruffled him up a little. He giggled. "May I ask where we are going, Divinity?"

"Oh! They didn't tell you?"

"They did not."

"We are going to … mingle with the lower classes."

#

The bearers moved swiftly. When they came to a stop, we stepped out in an alley. There were insulae on either side; some were burned out, others still stood. "Oh," said the Divinitas, "it's filthy here. Deliciously filthy."

He took my hand. "But is this safe?" I said, alarmed.

"We have people. Everywhere. There is never danger.

The God has watchdogs." He pulled me along.

Down a side alley and into another. The smells! Sausages and sewage. Vats of urine waiting for the laundry collectors. And people. People of every size and colour. The night was alive.

A food stall with a counter, round openings with earthen pots sunk into them, warmed by charcoal from below. Steaming entrées in the pots, and some jugs of wine behind. A bored slave stood there to take the order.

The Emperor chose some octopus fried in garam and honey, wrapped in a flatbread.

"It's one as, sir," said the vendor.

The Divinitas chuckled and whispered to me, "Actually, I haven't any money. I quite forgot!"

"No credit," said the slave. "We don't serve riff-raff."

"Riff-raff?" The Divinitas raised an eyebrow.

The slave shrugged. "I'll call my dominus," he said.

The Emperor scratched his ear. Then I saw the Praetorians, standing in the shadows. I fished a dupondius from my pouch and handed it over. The slave pushed over an as. The Divinitas picked it up. In the torchlight he examined it. "Uncle Gaius?" he said, referring to the one known familiarly as Caligula. "I thought his coins were all recalled." He wolfed down his octopus. He did not offer me any, even though I had paid for his food.

"Come on," he said. "Enough food."

"Some wine?" the slave said.

"At the next stop," said the Divinitas. He pulled me along as though we were schoolchildren.

A tiny doorway opened and a beefy arm emerged, pulling us inside. A corridor, barely wide enough for the

Emperor to go through sideways … and we emerged in a dingy room.

Against a mural with a pastoral theme, with a lot of nymphs shepherds and even a few sheep, there were couches set, and women of all shapes and sizes were lounging about. A few boys, too, and in one corner a well-oiled man in a loincloth brandishing a gladius. Nothing extraordinary. So it had been in the house of Petronius, when he was putting on a big party. Looking closer, I could see that they wore little signs around their necks. One said, "Lucia fellat" — Lucia performs fellatio. One tiny boy had a sign that read "Mentula magna." Presumably his organ was way out of proportion to his height.

"A lupanar," I said softly.

"Yes, a brothel. If Petronius hadn't picked you, this is where you'd be working. Your culus would be permanently gushing like an aqueduct."

I shuddered.

Presently, a proprietor of the lupanar emerged from an inner room. This was an older but still beautiful woman, her face so smoothened by lead white that it was more porcelain than skin. Her withered arms showed her true age. When she saw Himself, she started to prostrate herself.

"None of that, Clytaemnestra," said the Emperor. "I want to be an ordinary person tonight."

"Ah. You are here … anonymously," said the madam. "Well done, my Lord. You've managed to fool every meretrix in my establishment." She waved at all the prostitutes, and they waved back, jiggling, wiggling and giggling as they waved. Clytaemnestra told the Divinitas,

"Take your pick."

The meretrices laughed and ignored him.

'They *really* don't recognize you," I whispered.

"They'll regret it when they're strung up on crosses tomorrow."

"Patience, my Lord," I said. "This only shows how brilliant you are at the art of disguise."

Himself whipped round and glared at me. *Glared!* I remembered watching Marcus crucifying the pirates who kidnapped me. Petronius tolerated my back talk, encouraged it even, thought it adorable. Suddenly I remembered that Nero owned me. Yes, I had a scroll of manumission and a freedman's cap.

But *freedom?* A cruel joke.

Nero's eyes transfixed me. I could almost feel the nails riveting my wrists. Then the God suddenly smiled. "So refreshing," he said, "your candour. You've saved this whole brothel from execution. Not to mention the vendor who called me riff-raff."

"He's being crucified?"

"It's the Praetorians; they are *so* devoted. To a fault, indeed. They're probably doing it now."

"Now?"

"Go on. You can still stop them."

"But ... *domine,*" I whispered, still trying to pretend he was a nobody and that I was that nobody's slave boy. "I can't leave you. You didn't bring any money!"

Himself the Divine Emperor laughed. Heartily. Of course he did not need money here. The proprietor knew who he was. *Everyone* knew. The Emperor needed no protection from a fancy-boy.

"Run along and stop the execution," he said to me. "I'll

be occupied for a while."

#

I slipped out of the lupanar and found myself in complete darkness. I felt my way along a damp wall to what I thought would be the right corner. There was a glimmer of light. I turned another corner and found myself in a quadrangle with a well. There was more light. People were holding torches. A crowd had gathered. Two soldiers were tying the octopus vendor to a cross. People were exciting, babbling jeering. Little boys hoisted up on their parents' shoulders. The mood was festive. The vendor was screaming.

"Stop!" I shouted. I couldn't be heard until I pushed my way up. I saw the vendor's face clearly. His terror was beyond imagining. This wasn't a fancy display cross. The man would be dying at eye level, able to look any passerby in the eye. I shoved the closest soldier and he merely slapped me away, like an annoying insect. But out of the corner of my eye, I saw Marcus in the shadows.

"Marcus Vinicius!" I shrieked.

Marcus emerged. The two soldiers stopped their work leaving the food vendor half hoisted, the cross at at an angle, the man dangling by his arms, his feet unbounded. He was howling.

"Himself says to stop the execution," I told him.

"Halt," Vinicius barked.

The soldiers let the ropes go slack. The cross landed on the flagstones with a crack. It was a good thing it had fallen wood first or a few bones would have been broken at least.

The crowd got ugly fast. "We have to string him up," said one of the soldiers. "You can't promise a spectacle and not deliver."

Quick thinking was needed. "Listen to me!" I screamed. "I'm an emissary of Himself, your Emperor and God, and he has sent me in his Divine Compassion to stay this execution!"

The crowd was roaring with laughter until Vinicius hold up his hand. Then, lifting my arm high, he cried, "All hail the Divine Nero, Lord of Compassion! Listen to his words, brought to you from the lips of the Emperor's most trusted catamitus!"

They untied the poor man and he was still in a state of abject terror, but they soldiers gave him a quick boot in the buttocks and he scampered off, gibbering. The crowd's anger turned to cheering and shouts of "Vivat Caesar!" and even murmurs about me, as in "The Emperor's boy ... plucky little thing ..." and so on.

"Nothing more to see," one of the soldier's told the crowd.

"I'll take you back to the lupanar," Vinicius said. Her escorted me back, but did not enter."

#

They treated me differently this time. I was still wearing the same rags, but now the whores treated me like a prince, fawning and stroking my hair. At length Clytaemnestra emerged from an inner room. "Back to work," she said, shooing the girls and boys from the antechamber.

"Sit," she said, pushing me down onto one of the couches. "Himself will be occupied for a time. Amuse yourself with anyone you like. Here." She gave me a fistful of lead tokens. They were like coins, but each bore an image of some sexual act. "Himself never needed money here," she said. "These *sprintiae* are the currency in this establishment. Look them over. I'm sure there's something you'd like to try."

"I don't want a whore," I said. "I'll just wait."

"Have it your way," said Clytaemnestra. "But you'll be bored, though. I have clients I have to see to." She stood up. "I'll send a slave to keep you company. Maybe the bookkeeper; she's done counting the money for the night."

Clytaemnestra left and I was alone in the chamber. I sat in the light of a single oil lamp. I gazed at the mural. The nymphs seemed to dance in the gloom. From rooms beyond I could hear giggles, moans. I could feel myself dozing off.

Then I heard a voice.

A voice so familiar, I almost thought … "Mother?" I whispered.

She smiled. It was not my mother but it was as close as I could get on this earth. She stood there, a little older, her face more lined, but her eyes were as I remembered them. A familiar face, someone who had known me before I became … this.

"Sporus," she said softly. "You've come far since we buried your friend Hyacinth."

I embraced her then, the woman who had cleaned me up after I had been viciously raped by the pirate captain, the woman who had taught me my first words of Greek, the woman who had given me the shard of the bronze mirror which had shown my my face for the first time, the woman I called Spider.

IX

JULIA AGRIPPINA

At most a year had passed since we had seen each other, yet time had taken a greater toll that I could have imagined. She was haggard. Between the she was sold to the brothel and the time she was banished to counting money, she had to take dozens of customers a day. She was not the cream, pampered and well dressed and on display for the senators; Clytaemnestra had the full range of offerings, and several secondary houses frequented by plebeians and even slaves. It was her lack of physical attractiveness that had sent her to the lower class brothel, where they had used and abused her like an old sack of grain. But it was the wear and tear, coupled with her ability to read and understand nnumbers, that had sent her back to the main house and this relatively painless job.

"I've missed you so much," I said to her.

She took me in her arms and I could not stop crying. I relived it all. The sound of the sea, the pitch and yaw of the pirate vessel, the agony of my violated body. And her comforting words. Though she was a slave herself, and still was,

"Look at you," she said. "The plaything of a god, and I still the lowliest of the lowly."

"Not to me," I sobbed.

I tried to cram everything that had happened to me into the little time I knew we could be alone. It all came tumbling out. Petronius. The lofty poetry and biting portraits of real people and the filthy doggerel that he had woven into his *Satyricon.* The emperor. Poppaea and her cheetah. Otho, the husband who used me to be able to be aroused by his wife. And the Divinitas. How I loved him, how I hated and feared him, how he had simultaneously given me everything and taken everything away.

Spider's tales were more mundane than mine. Being raped by strangers at all hours had become routine to her, just something to be survived by making her mind go far away. The bookkeeping was a different routine; the tedium was a relief from the days of horror.

In the less busy hours, when few of the rooms were occupied, she told me, she swept the rooms and cleaned off the stains, for bodily fluids were shed in plenty in this business.

"Come with me on my rounds," Spider said. "It's a slow night, and there are Praetorians undercover all around here, making sure the Divinity takes his pleasures uninterrupted."

We took a steep stairway to an upper story. Small rooms lined a hallway, each one a cubiculum, barely wider than the couch it contained. Some had drapes drawn over the entry. In the others sat all manner of flesh. "Here are the snacks." She indicated a room where sad delicati sat naked. One emerged and handed Spider a fistful of coins. We walked past closed cubicula from which grunts, moans, and cries could be heard. "These are the main courses," she told me. There were voluptuous women. One, a Briton, was painted entirely blue. There were stylus-thin men and steatopygous matrons. We ascended another stair. "On to the more exotic fare," Spider said.

Each floor was more exotic than the last. Women dressed as gladiators, wielding whips. A fat old man in senatorial toga being humiliated by a slave. A bath of eels.

As the building was structured like one of those insulae that slum-dwellers live in, there were numerous flimsy stories; I was a little nervous that the constant shaking from the amorous activities would topple the whole building. Spider could see my unease.

"The Romans are good at building," she whispered.

"Yes," I said, "as long as it's stone and concrete."

I remembered the burning city. I remembered the Divinitas's poetic interlude. I remembered the Christians, dipped in pitch, lighting up the gardens, screaming.

"It will soon be *all* stone and concrete," Spider said. "Even at the edge of civilization, we hear the talk of Neropolis, and the new Golden House that will spring up from the ashes."

We went up to the sixth level and there was a bare room there. No furniture at all. "I call this room Olympus," Spider said. "We are above it all."

"And we don't have to think about any of it," I said.

"Not true."

She crouched on the floor and told me to do the same. I saw now that there were holes in the floor. Peepholes. Each was connected by an angled pipe into a room on a lower floor. Each hole had a circular covering of polished glass.

"Peer down one of the holes," she said. "This device was devised by some Greek academic. It makes things that are far look closer."

I knew the Emperor loved to look at the world through a polished ruby or emerald; he had even given me such a gem as a gift. If someone had invented a way to make faraway objects look closer, surely it could be put to better use than to observe lewd couplings in a brothel!

I lay down and put my eye up to the nearest opening. I could see into one of the cubicula, more elegantly appointed than the others.

A beautiful woman was reclining, her back to me, her face just outside the peephole's field of vision. She did seem to almost be in the same room. It was uncanny.

"That's the best peephole of all," Spider said, "just like the Divinitas's balcony at the circus, where you can smell and even sometimes taste the blood. This channel links directly to the Emperor's private room. You will see something provocative, I am sure."

And I did.

The woman turned around and her face moved into the center of the circle of light. At first I gasped, because I thought I had seen myself, but of course, it was not me. It was Herself, the Lady Poppaea Sabina, Empress of Rome.

Her face had been whitened with lead paint. Her lips were dyed crimson. Her eyes were accentuated with deep kohl. She was brandishing a little quirt. Not the kind you would use on a slave. This looked like something that could deliver a piquant little thwack, rather than real damage.

"I didn't expect *you* here," she said, play-acting.

Then came a voice from the shadows. An all too familiar voice. "I came to say I'm sorry. I didn't mean to ... kill you."

"You miserable little boy," she murmured, "You deserve a beating."

"Mother, mother, I've been bad..." Himself sounded whiny and uncertain.

The Empress whipped the air.

"I'm going to have to beat you, Lucius," she said.

The Emperor hove into view. He was naked. He was trembling. He seemed genuinely frightened. "And afterwards," he said, "can I have some milk?"

The Lady Poppaea unfastened her fibula with a single deft movement, and her stola slowly unravelled and slipped down her smooth, whitened flesh, toward the wooden floor.

"Get ready," she said, "for the thrashing of your life."

"Mother," he said.

"Who am I?" said the Empress.

"Mother!"

"What am I?"

"The Divine Julia Agrippina," he gasped.

"Suckle," she commanded. "For I am Agrippina. I am the all-omniscient mother. I am back from the dead. I shall haunt you forever."

The stola was in a heap on the floor, and the Divine Empress stood fully naked, and very obviously pregnant.

"But Mother ... you're with child. This isn't in the

game."

"I *am* with child! You're a bad boy and I shall make a new Lucius," she said, still playing her role.

"How dare you!" Nero shouted. "I killed you! You're just a ghost!" He lashed out with his fists. She dodged and struck back with the quirt. They were both yelling incoherently.

"I've had enough of this, Lucius. Call the boy."

Then the Emperor turned his back and stared up the ceiling, straight up to the narrow opening of the tunnel I was looking down. Did he know I was there?

"Sporus!" he screamed. He wasn't a god. He was a petulant child who wanted a new toy.

"Go to him," said Spider. *"Now."*

X

SATURN DEVOURING HIS CHILDREN

I ran down to the Imperial Cubiculum, almost tripping on the narrow steps. Spider led the way but she did not enter. Two men stood guard. Inside the chamber — the only one that had a door and not just a drape — the Divinity was shrieking my name.

"Sporus! Bring Sporus or I'll have you all crucified!"

I burst into the chamber.

"Sporus! Sporus! O Ganymede, cupbearer of Jove — that is to say, *my* very own cupbearer!" Himself, Master of the World, hurled himself at me, clutched and held me hard to his bosom — I was almost choking on his perfume — and covered my face and neck with kisses. He ripped my tunic and starting working his way down my shoulders, my chest, handling me like a child's toy.

"Divinitas!" I whispered.

It was not, I must admit, unpleasant to have the owner of

the known world slobbering all over me. I had not had any physical release for some time, not since the equally unexpected encounter in the palace when the Emperor had suddenly commanded me to mount him. Himself had not even reached my thighs before I was overcome by — that pinnacle of passion that the poet Sappho called *the mountain wind* – and all my pent-up desires came gushing out in milky profusion all over the God's face.

He did not back away but began laughing — well, alternately laughing and lapping — playing first the kitten, then the hyena. He clenched both my buttocks in his hands and, losing my balance, I fell backwards onto the couch and right onto the very pregnant body of the Lady Poppaea Sabina.

"Oh! I am so sorry, Goddess!" I said, for she still held the quirt in her hand. The Lady Poppaea shrugged.

"Well, *you're* a welcome relief," she said. "I thought I was done for."

I was not sure how to respond.

But she went on. "The Emperor's consumed with guilt about Agrippina, and who can blame him? And I'm stuck with the brunt of the guilt. You'd think he'd be a little more considerate, what with my condition. But his mother consumes his thoughts. And why shouldn't she? He murdered her, you know. It took three tries. You'll find out. Wait till you see him drunk. He'll think nothing of kicking you to death, and you haven't got any leverage to fight back with. You're not even a patrician."

"Guards!" Nero shouted. "Remove the Empress!"

The Praetorians entered and lifted Poppaea off the couch. They carried her off unceremoniously. They averted their eyes, though I for one would have been hard pressed to avoid staring at the spectacle of their God, his face soaked in my accidental discharge, his arms having slid from my rear and His Divine Person all jumbled up on the floor of this tawdry house of *infames*. When they left, Himself snatched what remained of my ripped tunic and swabbed at his face.

I helped him onto the couch. My copious education at the hands of voluptuaries and poets had not prepared me to deal with a raving Emperor.

I took the torn cloth and wiped his face a little more. There was no water in the room, so I urinated into the wad of fabric a little to clean it, then dabbed at his face a little more.

"I don't want a little Nero popping out of that woman," he said. "I don't need a successor. I'm a God."

"Then you don't have to have a successor, my Lord," I said. "The Gods go on forever."

"But they don't *rule* forever," said Himself. "Look at Saturn, for instance. He devoured his own children, and Jupiter *still* managed to claw his way out of his belly. And where is Saturn now? Imprisoned in Tartarus for all eternity."

"You won't end up in Tartarus, Divinitas. How could you? With all that great poetry you've written. You're like Orpheus, making the stones weep."

"I am, aren't I?" said Himself.

"Yes, Divinitas."

He held me close once more. He was hateful. And vulnerable. In that moment, I both loathed and pitied him. He stroked my hair, with an aching tenderness that confused me even more.

Then abruptly he turned away, let go of me with such

suddenness that I fell back down on the coach, banging my head a little on the frame, making me yelp; he ignored that. Petronius would have kissed it better.

"Orpheus was torn to pieces by drunk, insane women," he said.

There were, I am sorry to say, gaps in my knowledge of the exploits of the Greek and Roman gods. I had not heard that part of the story. But I knew that the cult of Orpheus had mysteries and initiations. For now, I could not comfort the Emperor with another tidbit of mythology.

"Agrippina!" the Emperor cried out. There was despair in his cry, heartbreak.

I could not assuage his grief with words, but I found another use for my tongue. He sobbed as he throbbed, the hurt and the ecstasy coming together in a place beyond my understanding.

***

Sordid! Beyond sordid!

Yet these are the things you've been dying to hear since I started this sorry narration.

I had hoped that mating with a God would be a somewhat more elevating experience.

I've had two Gods, you know. Not to mention an Almost-God, who missed the throne by just a few inches.

And which God was your favorite?

The Divine Nero was as good as it ever got. Elevating experiences? You need true love for that, and for true love you need both *eros* and *agape.*

Yet you did love Himself, the one who is now the object of Damnatio Memoriae. *In a very real sense, you will be dying for him.*

Yes.

We'd better get you back into makeup, Empress. It's running again, and there's another delay in your big moment, I hear. The managed to get the giraffes off stage, but now the elephants are stampeding. Can you hear them? Animals are really more trouble than they're worth. Children, too. When there's a crowd of Christians to be eaten, the young ones ruin the whole show. Too easy to get the mob on their side, and then where's the entertainment?

Oh, the Christians! I have stories about them, as well. When the Emperor disguised himself and went among the plebs, it wasn't just brothels he visited. We managed to get smuggled into one of their so-called love-feasts once. He wanted to know what they were really like, you know. A twinge of guilt? Or just curiosity? The God I worshipped and abhorred was a complex being.

And the Chrestianoi?

They're not what people think. Their rituals are pretty dull. No human sacrifice at all.

Well, that's rather boring. I'd rather hear more about naughty things in high places.

And you will.

Are you done yet? You've sat on this latrina for an hour. Here, I'll sponge you off.

Why? So you can tell your grandchildren that you once touched a place that a God once touched?

You are too funny, Sporus. I mean … Your Imperial Majesty.

I am going to be killed horribly in front of thousands of people. I think I'm entitled to a few bad jokes.

XI

THE WOMB THAT MADE THIS MONSTER

It must have been morning when I awoke. The cubiculum smelled of sweat, overripe perfumes, and bodily fluids, but I was alone. The Divinitas was nowhere to be seen. Oh ... not so alone after all. A woman, hunched over, was scrubbing vomit from a corner. It was Spider. When she noticed me stirring, she came to me and proffered a bowl of some clumpy porridge.

"Do I have to go back to the palace?" I said. It was the last thing I wanted to do. I would have stayed in the brothel if I could. At least here I knew where I stood. I could be a whore among whores.

"Perhaps not right away," Spider said. "The Emperor has been quite worn out by the night's entertainments. I'm sure he'll send for you and the Praetorians will know where to look."

"But I left Hylas there at the palace. A lamb among wolves."

"He has a lot more experience at being a slave than you," she said. "We are good at survival."

Indeed, Hylas was already at the door, and he held out a steaming posset in an earthenware bowl.

"How did you know where I was?" I asked him.

He laughed. "Me slave," he said. "Slave know everything."

"Ego," I said, *"Ego,* not *me.* I should really beat more grammar into you."

"Now you like a real dominus," he said, grinning from ear to ear, perfectly confident I would never lay a hand on him.

"But seriously," I said, "I will buy a tutor for you. It may become useful for you not to sound like you're only good at moaning and making eyes."

"Yes, domine," he said, using the vocative case properly for the first time. I knew that he knew I noticed. I knew that he had taken the effort for my sake. And in these little ways he showed me that he loved me. "But, domine," he went on, "can't we go home?"

"I think we can," I said. Hylas and Spider helped me to my feet. Hylas had fresh clothing, a woollen tunica and a purple-bordered toga praetexta, which was really only proper for a young Roman male of senatorial rank, or a boy of aristocratic birth who had not yet reached formal adulthood. I did not feel that I belonged to either category, and I demurred; besides, it is a heavy garment, and Rome can be sultry, and even months after the fire, the air was oppressive.

I said a quick goodbye to Spider, but I knew I would see her again. I knew that the underbelly of Rome would beckon to the Divinitas, whether he was in a Senate hearing, listening to old men with no power rambling on about minutiae; or whether he was enjoying a banquet with too many dishes, or a concert with too many notes; or whether he was merely in a depression, haunted by memories of his dead mother. At these times, I could tell, the dark side of the city would call out to him. He wanted so much to mingle with the ordinary, but he never could be ordinary. I wondered when the next summons to the palace would come, and whether Himself, in an insomniac wanderlust, would even find his way into my chamber, and find me missing.

My destiny was not my own. I would have to move back there. But maybe not for a few more days...

#

It was as a kind of master of the house that I returned to the home where I had once been Petronius's slave. Not the real master of course, but certainly a kind of conquering hero, for I had survived the summons to Himself's inner sanctum.

Croesus bowed to me and led me to the triclinium where slaves immediately brought olives, bread, salt, and wine. The simple food came as a relief after a surfeit of peacocks' brains and larks' tongues and such.

Some of Petronius's women slaves embraced me and made much of me. They wanted to hear my stories and for an hour or more I told them the same tales I have been telling you, tormentor of my final hours.

But soon it was time for *me* to ask questions.

"Hylas has already told me," I said, "how slaves know

everything. Since being freed, I've lost that ability. But more than ever, I *have* to know everything. I'll never survive Himself." And I talked about how I had been watching through the spyholes in the upper room, and I'd seen Himself actually kicking and beating the Empress in a rage. And what she said to me — that I'd have even less to defend myself with, since I'm not even of noble birth. "How will I stop him from kicking me to death, just for the momentary rush of it?"

"You need to understand the women who truly have power over him," Croesus said, "and how and why they wield that power. And you need to understand what love means to a God. And you need him to love you. You must do it by guile, by misdirection, and by understanding him so well that he could make his wishes real before he even thinks of them. Because someone like Nero does not *love.* My master, Gaius Petronius, *did* love you, Sporus. Hyacinth loved you. Hylas loves you blindly and desperately, savoring any second that you might have for him. In her own way, the Lady Poppaea Sabina loves you. And her husband Otho ... if he were ever to return from being exiled to the governorship of Lusitania ... he would marry you in a moment. You are an exact duplicate of the person he loves, without the constant scheming and with the added benefit of a penis."

"But the Emperor does not love me," I said.

"He may think he does, but there are only three people he loves, I think," Croesus said. "This I have gleaned from a thousand overheard conversations at my master's banquets."

"But he doesn't limit his appetites to three."

"No. Not at all. He's penetrated freeborn boys, senators'

wives, and, it is rumored, the Vestal Virgin Rubria, even though if it were true it would bring untold calamity to the city. Well, someone who say that calamity has happened already ... luckily, I suppose, we have the Chrestianoi to blame instead. But as for the women he loves ... there is Actë, you know. She is a lowborn woman, perhaps even a slave, who loved Lucius Domitius Ahenobarbus, before he became Nero, heir to Godhood. No one knows where she is. She is somewhere in the palace. She is like a ghost, haunting the corridors. They say she'll come out into the light one day, to be with him in death."

I wondered whether I would ever meet her. "And Poppaea?" I said. "Does he love Poppaea?"

"Oh yes," said Croesus. "That's probably why he hurts her."

"He hurts her because she's not his mother," I said, remembering what I had overhead the night before.

"His mother is his greatest love. Even though he killed her. *Because* he killed her. They say he ripped open her womb so he could see what such a monster as Himself had come from ... but that's just slaves' talk."

And now I understood more about Himself than I had learned even from Petronius. And I knew that, for better or worse, my destiny was tied to that of the master of the world.

How I envied my slave boy, Hylas. Today, I hated my freedom. I had traded my slavery for a darker enslavement, enforced not by the lash but by the gnawing dread that every step was a misstep, every word a self-condemnation.

Croesus saved until last the news that I was already being sent for. It was something really big — an occasion of state. I supposed I would be on view with the best of the imperial possessions, like the perfect vase, the comeliest horse.

But I still had until morning, because Himself was still recovering from the previous night's excesses.

"I'll sleep with Hylas," I said. "Just Hylas."

Hylas smiled eagerly.

"And I mean *sleep,*" I added.

Hylas frowned. "Yes, domine," he said.

XII
FREEDOM IS SLAVERY

I did not have to return to the Imperial presence for a few days, because the summons required preparation. A big occasion of state, they told me, giving no details. But they were sending a tailor, and I was to have a new wardrobe, grander even than the items they had already chosen for me on my last visit.

At some point, the Emperor would think of me, and at that moment, I had better be in reach. I believed, however, that Epaphroditus, who knew his master's desires before Himself knew them, would have me brought to the palace in plenty of time.

The daily routine of an upper-class Roman always began clients showing up to request favours or consult or present gifts. Without an heir present in the house, Croesus, the freedman, suddenly found himself a powerful man, even though he had no actual power; for Marcus Vinicius had vested a level of his uncle's *potestas* in the former servant, to act as proxy.

So the morning was occupied with petitions, some of them quite strange; one of them, indeed, exactly like the situation in my patronus's *Satyricon,* where two young students of rhetoric were fighting over the legal ownership of a slave boy.

The atrium was not exactly *crammed* with suppliants, but there were several waiting around. Some had perhaps found other sponsors since my master's suicide. They were a desultory lot.

In Petronius's novel, Encolpius spends an amazing night of passion with the beautiful Giton, only to have his best friend Ascyltus claim the boy in the morning. Encolpius, full of profound certainty about his love after that wild night, thinks that the boy should decide. In the book, my former master uses the incident to make you think about the complexities of slavery in a way that never crosses most Roman minds, because Giton chooses the man who mistreats him and doesn't think of him as anything other than an object.

I wondered whether we would now see this fiction play out in real life.

But we did not. The boy in question was glum and past the usual age of a delicatus, with appalling acne. The young men were spoiled scions of my patronus's former clients, citizens but just a generation beyond slavery themselves. They both had various documents with vague references that *could* imply ownership.

"Isn't this something for an actual magistrate to decide?"

Croesus said.

They both started talking at once, and waving their certificates of title, or whatever the documents were.

"May I say something?" I asked. They were suddenly silent, looking at me as though I possessed some real authority. "Let the boy decide."

"That's outrageous!" both complainants said at the same time.

"He's a slave," said the one on the left. "He can't decide, by definition. He's not a person."

The "not-person" in question appeared more and more glum.

He was an unprepossessing thing but this whole transaction made me furious. A year ago I had been in as terrible a situation. Doubtless he had it worse than I ever did, because, with my looks, I was not the kind of merchandise anyone wanted to damage. When I looked at the two men competing for ownership, they revolted me. The scene from my former patronus's book was cheap and tawdry, but this did not even have the artistic veneer of being a literary satire — it was the thing itself, without an ounce of wit.

"Croesus," I said, "can I afford this boy?"

Croesus said, "Not only did you inherit quite a bit from your patronus, but you also, probably, have a direct line to the privy purse — in case you hadn't noticed."

"You can't buy him," said one of the putative owners, "until we've settled who owns him."

"Pay them both off," I said. Then, I asked the boy directly, "Which of these creatures do you choose, of your own free will?"

"Neither," he said firmly. "My father's a baker. He sold

me to *this* one to pay off a gambling debt. But I think he sold me twice. Well, he was supposed to sell my brother, too, for the *other* gambling debt, but this one —" he pointed to the other of the two — "got a bit violent. He's dead. The medicus says my brother's heart was weak. This man says he was given a damaged slave and wants me as compensation."

"You people are revolting," I said to the men. "Get out."

"Can I go home now?" said the boy.

"You want to return to the family who sold you off, twice?"

"Can't choose your family," the boy said. "But I *could* choose to go with someone else. I choose *you,* domine."

"I'm not a choice."

"Master, you've shown me more compassion than I've ever received in my entire life. Let me serve you. I'll lace your caligae. I'll suck your mentula."

Croesus shrugged. "Compassion," he said wryly, "is its own reward."

"Can you read and write?" I said.

"I do all the accounts at the bakery," he said. "My father never could count past X."

"I'll give you to Hylas," I said. "You will teach him to speak proper Latin, and you're to receive ten lashes if he misses a case ending."

"No, domine, no," Hylas said. "You *kill* him. Me have no case ending."

"Thank you, lord," said the boy, prostrating himself and slobbering over my right foot. "I don't mind the lashes. My father would beat me for charring a loaf."

"We won't be beating you for that sort of thing," I said.

"I know Greek, too," said the newly garrulous boy.

"And Aramaic. And Hebrew. I'm from Judaea, you know. My family was captured and sold when Pompey the Great came to Jerusalem. We've been in Rome for a hundred years."

Croesus slapped him. He grinned.

"I don't need your biography; I don't even even know your name," I said.

"Simon."

"Simon, this is Hylas. Teach him to talk like a civilized person."

"His speech will be as beautiful as his face, domine."

It seemed that my slave now had a slave.

That was another Roman paradox, I suppose. A slave is by law a thing, a blank tablet on which his dominus can inscribe any history, and personality. You cannot by definition rape a slave because that would imply the existence of a person inside that piece of flesh you violated. The death of Simon's brother had provoked no remorse at the unconscionable abuse that had caused it; it merely meant that this was a defective piece of merchandise to be compensated for….

And yet, Rome says that by a simple magical act of manumission, a person suddenly exists. And even without a person being present, there is still enough of a shadow of personhood to *possess* another non-person. Even though slaves, by definition, have no property.

There was, after all, no simple line dividing freedom from slavery.

Petronius once told me, Aristotle said that the worst thing about slavery is "that the slaves eventually get to like it."

I was free, now, wasn't I? I could go where I pleased,

dress as I wanted, even buy a slave.

But I could not go where I pleased, or dress as I wanted.

That afternoon, the tailor came from the palace, and I realized just how enslaved I still was. I was not getting a new wardrobe as such, but a series of new identities, to be switched back and forth according to the Divinitas's whim.

XIII
FOR FOR A QUEEN

Apparently, whatever this state occasion was, I was not to be presented as Sporus, the Divinitas's little plaything. The tailor had come with silks, which come from far beyond the edge of the Roman world, which is to say, *the* world. "Woven by the gods themselves," said the man, a Nubian dwarf named Leontes. Priceless rolls of cloth were being rolled out and draped on statues and columns.

"I know. You are expecting a fussy little Greek," he said, as slaves spread out even more fabrics in the triclinium.

A bust of Petronius stared down from a Corinthian base. Croesus had redecorated, bringing out all the images of our former master, so that he still seemed to inhabit the house.

"Not a fussy little Greek," I said, "I know that is just a silly stereotype. But somehow *you —"*

"And you would be right, domine," said Leontes. "I

could tell you that I was a prince in my country, but I imagine you've heard that before."

"Not just heard it — I've used that one myself."

We both laughed.

As his slaves (which included, indeed, a number of fussy little Greeks) measured me and prodded me and stuck lengths of sheer fabric on me with fibulae, he told me his story.

"It is true I was a prince, but I was born to a tribe that views deformity as witchcraft," he said. "But a buyer for the games came to the village, scouting for dwarfs; he had a tableau in mind, amazons in chariots drawn by ostriches, battling dwarfs in heavy armour. My father the king traded me for a dozen oxen, and was glad of the bargain. Yet, though I looked the part, I could not handle a gladius to save my life. Instead of exercising with wooden swords, I spent my time with the kitchen and household slaves, and eventually the lanista noticed that our gladiators were decked rather more elegantly than those of other gladiatorial establishments. Nothing much, but I marshalled the resources of the school to add a fold here, a tuck there, a little ornament, so that our winners looked more triumphant, and our losers at least died with dignity. Oh, I did slay the odd amazon, but eventually the senator who owned the school realized I was of more use elsewhere. You did not see the Empress Messalina's wedding gown! That was mine. A month of little stitches!"

This autobiographical chatter engaged my interest in spite of myself. I could well imagine that, if I had not had my looks, I too could have been fodder for the arena ...

#

As you are now.

Don't remind me.

As if you need reminding, my Empress, my Divinity.

#

The dressmaker's chatter did have the effect of distracting me, because the more pieces of cloth they wrapped me in, the more worried I became. I started thinking I was being wrapped for burial. Indeed, in a sense, being prized object of beauty in the palace was a kind of living death.

"It's a shame about the genitalia," Leontes said. "They rather ruin the holistic outlines this sheer fabric draws in the air about you."

"Pity you can't just cut them off," I said.

#

I bet you regretted those *words.*

You cannot imagine how often I replayed that scene in my mind. An offhanded bit of sarcasm that might have sealed my fate. But who was to know? Perhaps Leontes did not have the ear of the Divinitas. Perhaps the Emperor conceived it all himself. There was, after all, no limit to his cruelty.

Nor, at times, his love.

#

I had tried on a dozen pieces of finery when I realized I had seen some of these clothes before. "Aren't these Poppaea's?" I said.

Leontes mumbled something.

"You are ignoring me."

I recognized some of the pieces. And one fibula, in particular, I was sure I had seen it. It was a lapis lazuli carved into the shape of a rampant lion, with a mane of gold.

"These clothes *are* Poppaea's," I said.

"And we have to be quick, before they are missed," said the dwarf. "The Divine Poppaea is at some Magna Mater shrine, celebrating the mysteries, but she will be back before the tenth hour."

"Why am I supposed to be wearing her clothes?"

"Can you not posture in such a boyish manner, domine? You'll ruin the effect."

"What effect?"

"My dear domine, can you turn that wrist more daintily? Can you not stampede about the room like a raging adolescent lad?"

"Is that not what I am?"

"You will play a role, domine. And if you don't do it well, it will fare badly for us, as well."

Realizing that their fates as well as mine rested on my performance, I sat still while they padded my hips and chest a little, and while a cosmetician applied painted my face with delicate strokes, and two others teased and piled my hair.

And presently I found myself looking at my reflection in a mirror of polished bronze and I was transformed. My hair was elaborately coifed and elaborated extended with a tall wig. Exotic fabrics caressed my skin, and an outer layer of rich purple left no doubt as to my Imperial status. The fibula I recognized was holding it all together at one shoulder. Lead white gave my face an unearthly pallor and my lips were stained blood-crimson.

I stood taller. Arrogance flecked my lips. I felt ennobled. Entitled, indeed.

I was not just the Divine Poppaea Sabina, Mistress of the

World. I was an idealized version of the Empress. And I have to admit that, in these garments, my way of moving, my way of walking, shifted towards the feminine. It was instinctive. I never felt beautiful as a boy, but as a woman, as an Empress …

Perhaps it was just a role, but I was pulling something from deep within myself.

Or was it simply that I had no identity? That I was merely a shard of mirror, reflecting the fantasies of others?

XIV

THE KING OF ARMENIA

And thus it was that I stepped, radiant as the sunlight, from my litter, and ascended onto a gilded bier drawn by white horses. Horse-drawn *anything* is illegal in Rome during the daytime — whether it's carts of merchandise or a general's chariot, which meant that wherever I was going, it had to be a major event indeed.

On this bier was a throne, and crouched on the steps were my slaves, Hylas, more friend than slave now, if he only knew it, and the Jew I had recently acquired by accident. I was greeted by Epaphroditus himself. The Emperor's secretary glowering at me was another indication that this was no ordinary occasion.

Epaphroditus said, "Now listen. You're not to say a single word. You're here as an illusion, an illusion *only*. Understand."

"An illusion, yes," I said, barely sensing I even had an identity under the layers of fabric and cosmetics.

The entire contraption started to move. The horses were

not used to the narrow street. One whinnied and reared up. At once, someone else, who had been behind the throne, so I did not notice him before, came lunging out. It was the boy philosopher Epictetus, and he was struggled to hold on to the cheetah Hercules, who looking like he was about rip his flimsy gold chain.

Hercules sprang into my arms as Epictetus was forced to let go. Simon screamed. Epictetus stumbled and tripped over the step. He got up. He was limping.

"Ah," Epaphroditus said, "Hercules remembers you — that's a relief."

I stroked the cheetah. "He should know me," I said. "We shared a box once." The animal had been liberally perfumed. I am sure that it was the scent that was driving him mad. "Why is Epictetus limping?"

"He is always getting himself knocked about," said Epaphroditus.

But I suspected there was more to it than that.

Presently the horses came under control and the entire tableau, with me enthroned and the boys and a cheetah at my feet, started moving downhill.

"Since I am not to say a word, Epaphroditus," I said, "Would you please tell me what role I am to play at least?"

"Isn't it obvious?" said the Emperor's secretary. "You are to be the Divinitas, the mistress of the world. You will be fine if you don't talk. Or at least, just stick to pleasantries."

"But where is the *real* Poppaea?"

"The Lady Poppaea Sabina is indisposed today. But you knew that. She is with child and she has been feeling poorly for days. She doesn't feel like sitting in the hot sun for an endless coronation."

"Coronation?—" My panic must have shown. "Surely Poppaea is Empress already."

Epaphroditus laughed. "You actually thought …" Even my slaves tittered. They must have already heard some gossip. "No, no, my empty-headed little sweetmeat, you will not be crowned queen quite yet! This is the coronation of Tiridates, King of Armenia, at the hands of his overlord, the King of the Universe."

Simon winced. "Among our people, we only use that title for the one true god," he murmured.

Epaphroditus grunted. "Monotheists! Better not say that in front of the Emperor."

Our little cortège had grown a little. Bucinae and tubae were blaring to the steady rhythms of slaves each beating a hand-held tympanon. At the foot of the hill the street widened a little and now it was lined with onlookers. Hercules was nervous at so many people and I was constantly stroking him.

We were approaching the forum. The crowd grew, and now soldiers stood on either side, preventing them from getting too close. We were moving down the Via Sacra, with the Temple of Peace to our right, about to reach the Temple of Castor and Pollux. People watching me go by weren't entirely enthusiastic.

An egg flew at me, missing the throne but catching Simon on the nose. "You murdered Octavia!" someone shouted.

I started to say I had nothing to do with that.

Another missile, this time a rotten cabbage. It hit Hercules, who became agitated. It was all I could do to hold on to the golden leash.

"Not a word!" Epaphroditus hissed.

"Boys, help me keep Hercules under control," I said. Simon and Hylas struggled between the two of them to keep Hercules from becoming too agitated. Meanwhile, Epictetus limped over to me with a small sack of coins.

"They'll calm down once you throw some of these around," he said.

I reached into the bag as a hunk of stale bread narrowly missed my head. Now I had a handful of coins — nothing less than a denarius, and even a few aurei. I started tossing them. The crowd switched almost instantly from abuse to cheering. A child dived through the line of soldiers at an aureus, only to have his hand stomped on by a pair of metal-studded caligae. He squealed as he was kicked back.

I wanted to help him, but the procession had already moved on. In this city that had adopted me, violence was casual and not worth anyone's notice.

I hardly had time to react to the change from being reviled to being lionized, for at that moment a nauseating stench assailed my nostrils. We were about to cross the Cloaca Maxima, a miracle of Roman ingenuity, the vast sewer into which all of the city's waste flowed before being flushed to an outfall beyond the walls. The aqueducts, the vast public baths, the intricate system that supplied the city, eventually led here. The whiff hung heavy in the sultry air; for the greater a city, the greater its production of shit.

When we crossed the Cloaca Maxima, the odor quickly fell away, or rather blended into the myriad smells of the Forum. The baking, the body odors, the grilling, the slaughtering of small animals at altars, made for a kaleidoscope of stenches, sucking up and blending into the reek of the Cloaca.

Many more soldiers now, lined up with their tall shields forming four walls. Behind them, the crowd; slaves and senators, grandmothers with infants in their arms, children on the shoulders of grownups. A blast of a consort of bucinae and wailing tones of a water-organ.

A dais had been raised up in the center of the Forum. Statues of the gods looked down from every side, vividly painted, glaring down on the world of mortals, yet the god on the throne was not painted marble. A monument himself, encased in purple and gold, Himself looked upon me as I descended. My slaves escorted me to a lesser throne, to the right of Himself, as befit my status as a lower deity.

Epaphroditus bowed deeply to the Emperor and said, "I have brought the Lady Poppaea Sabina, the Empress, to attend the ceremony as you commanded."

Nero barely looked at me. "I'm glad you've changed your mind, my dear," he said.

"Not a word!" Epaphroditus whispered in my ear as I took my seat. I smiled wanly. The weight of the robes, the stickiness of the face paint, the searing summer heat, were all making me run with sweat. Even through the perfume, surely the Divinitas would know the difference between the scent of a man and a woman. Yet he seemed oblivious.

Perhaps because the smell of the cheetah, despite his perfume, was more overpowering than mine.

"My wife," said the Divinitas, and now I saw for the first time that there was a man prostrate on the ground in front of the Emperor. Many were prostrate in fact, but this one wore enough gold ornaments to purchase a small city. As this man rose to a kneeling position, I could see his face clearly. He had the complexion of someone from the East, Parthia or Arabia Felix, perhaps, and was bearded in the eastern fashion — most Romans prefer shaving their facial hair — and had an imperious bearing, much like Nero himself.

Yet he spoke with humility. "As I have performed the *proskynesis* before you, my Emperor and God, I also humble myself before you, O Goddess," he said, smoothly returning to his prostration, this time before me. "Forgive me if your beauty blinds me a little."

"Enough of that," said the Emperor. He waved, and a slave presented the Divinitas with a crown on a silken cushion.

"You have shown me that you and yours belong to me, and that Armenia is properly beholden to me, and to Rome," said the Emperor. "And in acknowledgment that you have accepted our overlordship, we are most pleased to return to you the crown of Armenia, Tiridates."

He placed the crown on Tiridates's head.

The cheering that surged around us was not compelled. Nero Claudius Caesar Augustus Germanicus was loved in those days.

#

And still is, if history were written by the common people.

That is true. If the mob had their way, you would not be facing a grotesque death right now.

Yet they'll enjoy my death very much, I am sure.

They are fickle.

There are those who deny that he has died, I hear.

That is true. How many Emperors have ruled so far this year, three, four? Yet they still long for those carefree days of poetry, chariot races, and lions eating Christians. I think there's going to be a little bit of that as an appetiser to your big scene, actually. But people find that sort of thing boring now. The Christians are no fun; they are far too compliant.

If my execution keeps getting delayed, I may yet have time to tell of how the Divinity and I infiltrated one of their notorious love-feasts.

I can't wait!

In time. I must finish telling you of Tiridates.

#

I stood there, a few steps lower than the Divinitas, and the Armenian King between us. The cheering was overwhelming.

"This evening," the Divinitas said, "we'll have some spectacular private games as well as a banquet. And then," he went on, "perhaps I and the Empress will entertain you in private."

I dreaded to think what Nero meant by "entertain."

"Divinitas!" Tiridates exclaimed.

"Poppaea can be quite excitable when she's had too much wine," said the Emperor, turning to acknowledge the cheers. "You did say you were blinded by her beauty, did you not?"

"But is she not with child, Divinitas?"

"Oh, pregnant women can do plenty," he said, smiling.

I bit my tongue. I knew why Epaphroditus had told me to say nothing. The Emperor was in one of his moods. Perhaps he was brooding about his mother again. Was this why Poppaea had not wanted to be present?

Had something happened to Poppaea?

Did the Emperor even realise that I was not his wife?

The Emperor put his arms around me and kissed me

playfully on the cheek. "Don't give yourself away," he whispered sweetly, "or I'll cut off your testiculi and feed them to the peacocks." He turned to Tiridates, all smiles, and waved at the crowd again. I waved, too, and got a massive cheer.

The Emperor had known all along.

XV

THERE ARE NO EQUALS

After the crowd had thundered itself raw, the royal procession moved on to Campus Martius where stood the Theater of Pompey. The guests followed — of course, I mean important guests only, of course, no one below patrician rank — unless you happened to be a famous actor, musician, or gladiator, of course — in that case, even slaves welcomed.

I had not seen this place before but I knew that this was where the Divine Julius had been assassinated. But that was almost a century ago. Only fogeys and philosophers know that Rome was once a Republic.

When we entered the Temple of Venus Victrix, which forms the side of the theater from which the raked seating descends, it was all I could do to act unsurprised, for every piece of furniture, every column, every wall had been gilded. There was so much gold it was like gazing into the sun.

I look my place in the Empress's throne, my slaves struggling to keep Hercules on his leash. But once I sat, the cheetah crouched meekly at my feet.

As we sat, there was a battle between *andabatae* being staged to put the audience in a cheerful mood. These unfortunates wore helmets that covered their eyes, so they could not see anything, and were standing around swinging their swords, only occasionally blundering into a hit. They ran into walls and each other, and the audience was shouting at them, usually giving misleading directions. It was surprising that they could succeed in killing anyone at all, but eventually they all lay in a heap of blood and metal and were cleared away with hooks, with a man dressed as Pluto, Lord of Death, overseeing the slaves who had to drag off the bodies.

While they were cleaning up, Himself introduced me to his guest.

"Tiridates, King of Armenia," he said, "thanks to *my* Divine Intervention, I might add. My wife, the Empress."

Tiridates inclined his head. I detected the shadow of a smirk. Did he know?

"You look amazing," he said. "The rumors did not do you justice. And … in your condition, too."

"As a goddess," said the Divinitas, "my wife does not whelp like normal mortals. It's all magic. She doesn't have to be encumbered by a grotesque, kickable belly."

"Miraculous," said Tiridates. "Rome is fortunate to have living gods and goddesses."

I was getting a sinking feeling, but there was no way to escape. I was a puppet, and the world was the puppet theater.

"You find her attractive?" the Emperor said slyly.

"... Ah, how could I not, Divinitas?" said the King of Armenia.

"Take her for a night, if you like," said Nero.

"To profane a goddess! To blaspheme!" Tiridates whispered, his awe tempered with salaciousness.

"We are not governed by the same rules as ... men," the Emperor said, gazing pointedly at that part of my stola which should not have been concealing any kind of manhood.

At that rather awkward moment, I was rescued from my anatomy being scrutinized more closely because a huge fanfare on barbaric bucina-like instruments made from the horns of rams came blasting from the opposite within the Temple of Venus and Victrix and a cacophonous orchestra emerged, the horns in the vanguard and massive copper drums in the rear, and ear-splitting, screechy winds.

"I didn't order up a barbarian wind band," said the Divinitas, waving at Epaphroditus, who scurried out of the crowd with a scroll of program notes. "Send them away."

"By no means, Divinitas," said King Tiridates. "You've entertained me for days; let me show you an exhibition by some of our Armenian mages."

Nero seemed impatient. He never liked being upstaged, but I could see his was struggling to seem gracious. He must have his own show lined up, I thought, and didn't want to sit through an hour or two of Armenian choreography. This music did not seem pleasant to my ears — how much more painful to the Emperor, with his delicate sensibilities? He sat there, wrinkling his nose, while Tiridates applauded happily.

We sat through a succession of mages. They did things with fire; leaping through hoops, making flames shoot from their mouths, hands, and even buttocks, flames of different hues. A woman was placed in a sarcophagus and sawn in half, and the nether half walked away, her feet protruding from the coffin.

They were illusionists — sophisticated ones, tricks I hadn't seen in the marketplace. In spite of the bickering between the King and the God, I found myself entranced. The blaring music actually became bearable as time went on. And no one was being killed ... not even the woman sawn in half, who came back for a bow. That was a tremendous relief, because few entertainments in Rome were free of killing, even if it was just some hapless criminal being eaten in the background.

Looking over at the Divinitas, I could see that he was not really watching the conjuring tricks at all. He was clearly impatient to put on a show of his own. At length, Himself raised a hand and silence fell abruptly, the winds gurgling to a stop on a particularly ugly dissonance.

He waited. He was always the master at waiting for the utmost silence. One could, as they say, hear a fibula drop.

"O Tiridates," he said, turning to his guest with a languid arm gesture, "you have bewitched, nay, bedazzled us with the sophisticated illusions of Armenia's mages. Let me now repay you with a performance of my own."

Epaphroditus brought a golden lyre and a slave set up a gold sedilla as the mages, musicians, and dancing girls scurried out of the way. At the peripheries of the stage, slaves were still sweeping up some bloodied sand.

"Go sit with Tiridates, Poppaea, dear," he said to me. "That throne is ample enough, if you cuddle."

Trying to behave as if this was the most normal thing in the world, I crossed over to Tiridates's throne, cheetah in tow. He made room for me. It was, to say the least, awkward. It was a tight squeeze and

He advanced toward the seat, making every step an expression of divine hauteur. The hush was complete. Anticipation, indeed … but tinged with fear. Hercules tensed. He, of course, could smell it. He snarled. But silently.

The Divinitas played a single note on his lyre. Behind him, from hidden places, a hundred kitharas responded, echoing and reechoing that single note until in hung in the air like unformed dew.

And then he began to sing.

Yes, it was Niobe again, dreary Niobe mourning endlessly for her children, yet the fact that each of his melismas were picked up by strumming kitharas made the vast chamber an elusive shimmer of sound, waves of sound, like the sea … and I thought for the first time in an age about the sea, the salt scent hanging in the wind as though carrying my tears out over the emptiness.

"I know who you are," Tiridates said, his lips barely moving, his face set into a mask of adoration as Himself continued to sing. "I think that this entire spectacle is a scandal." He put his arm around me and let his hand wander down to where my breasts should have been. "Nice," he said, pretending to squeeze them, though he and I both knew there was nothing to squeeze.

And I? I went along with the charade. I knew Himself was watching, even as he sang his heart out.

"Is it true," he said, "what my spies tell me? That Himself kicked Poppaea in a fit of rage, and she is in too much pain to attend my coronation?"

"I really don't know," I whispered. "They don't really

tell me things." Was that what the Divinitas had meant, those chilling words about the Lady Poppaea's "kickable belly?" But I had seen them go at it, in the brothel that night. Indeed, I assumed that it was part of their lovemaking — the screaming match that would segue inevitably into a bout of wild sex.

"You really are everything they say, though," he said. "The whore shines brighter than his mistress."

"Reflected light," I said, "nothing else." I looked away. Was I really going to be gifted to this man for the night? Could I steal away later? There was bound to be a banquet. And in a banquet, people pass out. Even gods. I needed to look for Poppaea, to find out for myself if Himself had taken out his rage on her ... rage that I knew was really directed at his own mother, Agippina.

For a while, we listened to Himself. The sound of the kitharas was a tonal cushion on which his voice slithered like a viper, seductive and deadly. I felt the Emperor's song ... crawling into my robes, licking my bare skin. He did have power. He was not some bloated amateur as so many of you have suggested, who did not even hear him sing. I wondered how it was affecting the Armenian.

I realized I had already resigned myself to being handed out like a trophy. I found myself wondering whether the Armenian would be considerate, or whether he would hurt me.

"Do you want me?" I blurted it right out, not the most prudent way for a freedman to address a monarch, even a puppet king.

"He's already offered me fifty million sesterces," he said. "All that, and a queen, too? It's a test, I think. When you come to me in the middle of the night, and I presumably discover you aren't actually the Empress...."

"You won't be disappointed," I said. "No one ever is."

"I believe it. And yet —"

"Yet?"

"I'm not much for boys," Tiridates said. "I know, that's very quaint for a Roman to hear. But there's definitely a piquancy to who you are. Not just the boy-girl thing, but also the servant-mistress thing. You're the perfect love object, able to be all things to all lovers."

"Except to myself," I said.

"Don't think I don't understand how you feel," said the Armenian King. "I gave up *everything* to be here, and I do not know if it's worth it; my life, my kingdom subject to the whims of ... *that* ... just like you. It's unconscionable. Nero did not win my war. It was his man, Corbulo — a fine general, a skillful strategist. But it's Nero who owns me."

"But still, you're a king," I said.

"And kings can't always do what their penises tell them. Our *heads* must rule ... or else, they roll."

And before I knew it, I started to weep. Here, surrounded by Rome's elite, every eye aware of my every gesture, I felt utterly, entirely alone.

Until I became aware of Hylas. I had not even noticed him moving from my throne to crouch on the steps of the Armenian's. Hylas was expressing his feelings to me in the only way possible for a slave in such a public place. Gently, unselfconsciously, he was kissing my feet. I wished he could hug me as an equal, but in Rome, there are no equals.

XVI
THE NATURE OF TYRANNY

I could not be in tears for long. Tiridates leaned over and wiped my eyes with a fold of his kingly robe. "Not in public," he said softly. "You're a queen. The illusion is *everything.*"

Himself sang, his voice soaring in the silence, now and then punctuated by a ritornello from the massed kitharas. During these pauses, the Emperor peered at me. Or so it seemed. As though I were being singled out from this whole throng. I felt like an insect about to be crushed.

So I made it through the remainder of Nero's Niobe, a boy and a cheetah crouched at my feet, comforted by a king I barely knew.

The event ended with the Senate bestowing upon Himself the Divine Nero the title of Imperator, but what did a title mean when one was already a God? He received the newest honour with a languid wave. He summoned me to his throne and said, "You see that Tiridates is taken care of."

Later came the banquet, lit up by a few leftover Christians dipped in pitch, set aflame on towering crosses, had no surprises, not even its excess. It was a select event in one of the gardens. Though it was a spectacle beyond any previous banquet I had attended, its mood was desultory.

There were no poets. They were dead, or in exile. No Seneca, no Lucan, and of course, no Petronius; the world was so much darker now, with Himself its only literary luminary.

While there were no readings by great Latin poets ... there was plenty of entertaining violence, but no one was watching as the best-trained warriors in the empire fought to the death.

Interest perked up a little when Lucius Domitius Paris, the actor, did a little turn, but nothing so florid as Niobe; he knew better, perhaps, to compete with a God. In fact, he made a recitation from Aeschylus — one of the speeches of Prometheus, inveighing against the God for his punishment in daring to steal the gift of fire. I was sure that there was some hidden message in the choice of text and it certainly had an effect on Himself, who was the only person in the garden paying attention.

The Greek of Aeschylus is five hundred years before our time and bristling with weird archaisms, yet Paris was so convincing an actor that I thought I could understand every obsolete aorist and every arcane allusion. He imbued every syllable with its own melisma that illustrated what the word meant, so I needed no translation.

By now, it was getting dark, because the Christians had burned to a crisp and they had run out; most of the last batch had managed to elude execution by murmuring a prayer to Himself. Which is why no one really felt much pity for them; not acknowledging Himself puts the entire structure of the state at risk, and what is so wrong with a pinch of incense and a prayer? I have endured far worse, for the sake of survival, and I know deep inside that my true self is not touch. And what god is such a fool as to be unable to pierce the veil of hypocrisy and see what is in a man's heart?

I had got up from my dining couch and was circulating among other triclinia laid out in the garden, and I heard those exact sentiments from an old drunk man; I recognized him as Pontius Pilatus, and I recognized the stories, too — the orgiastic love-feast cults, the baby-eating and what not — from the last banquet I'd seen the old general at. But the way he told the stories was more … I would say, more mechanical, like a schoolboy reciting Homer, trying to get through the lines while avoiding the tutor's quirt.

"Ah," he said, greeting me, "Poppaea. Or are you Poppaea's evil twin? You've lost your baby belly."

"Still telling the same tall tales, General," I said. "But the telling isn't the same; this time, your tales are literally lighting up the banquet."

"It's a good thing they're using the display crosses," said Pilatus, "so we can get the light without the smell."

A woman sitting next to him said, "And without the guilt, Pontius."

"I daresay if they were marinated in garlic and garum instead of being coated with pitch, the smell would be quite pleasant," another guest piped up.

"The guilt," the woman said again, grimly lifting a

honeyed mouse by the tail and popping it her mouth, then spitting out the tiny bones.

"My wife, the Lady Procula," said Pilatus. "She used to have nightmares about it. Now, *I* have the nightmares."

"Because, my dear," said the Lady Procula, "you *know* they don't *actually* have baby-eating orgies."

"Blood rites, dear. They do have blood rites."

"Metaphorical, husband! They are a completely harmless cult. The Jews don't worship the Emperor either, and *they're* not lighting up his dinner parties."

"They will be soon," said another voice. Tigellinus, also making the rounds. "I hear they are revolting again."

He bowed to me.

"Not attending to the Divinitas?" I said, trying to sound imperious.

"I *am,*" he said testily. "I am doing my due diligence, keeping my eyes and ears open for seditious whispers."

"And if you find any?"

"I keep some pre-signed, blank death warrants on hand."

I moved away.

As I was, ostensibly, the Empress, I could not just slip away although there were so many things I wanted to find out. Where was Poppaea? Was she actually on death's door? Or were they just having a marital spat? After all, even Jupiter and Juno had them.

As I move among the guests, they paid me due deference. I am sure some of them knew. Paris, the actor, no longer playing Prometheus, was being harangued by the Divinitas.

"I want your tricks," Himself was saying. "You have tricks, I know you do. Only tricks could bring that hoary, antiquated windbag to life."

I knew that to Greeks, Aeschylus was almost as untouchable as Homer, and I imagine Himself knew it too. The master of the world was baiting the actor, and I knew it was from envy. I wondered if the greatest actor of our age would soon be going the way of Petronius, Seneca, and Lucan. The unassailable canon — Homer, Aescylus, Sophocles, Euripides, Sappho ... all of them, Petronius always said, were perfect. Even their imperfections were perfect.

So, when Lucius Domitius Paris did not directly spring to the "hoary, antiquated windbag's" defence, but merely stood with head bowed, I knew there was drama afoot, more drama even than the eagle devouring Prometheus's entrails.

Finally, the Emperor whispered a quote from the play itself: "Don't labour uselessly," he said, "at what can avail you nothing."

Paris said nothing.

"You don't think I can achieve those heights, do you?" said the Emperor. "You think my singing is mere vanity, a 'sickness rooted in the nature of tyranny'? That's what you were going to say, isn't it?"

"Divinitas," said the actor softly.

"Again, you refrain from the obvious riposte: 'it is best for a truly wise man to be thought a fool.'"

It was clear that Himself, the Divine Nero, was not Himself this evening. Or rather, perhaps he was *truly* Himself ... a terrifying notion for the one who was acting out the role of his bride.

I wished I could disappear into thin air. But instead, I spoke up. "Lucius, my dear," I whispered, taking his arm, every bit the steadying hand of the loyal wife who comes to the rescue of her drunk husband, "let's not be over-hasty. Look at the man — he's merely overwhelmed by your magnificence. He's done his very best, but his Prometheus isn't fit to undo the caligae of your Niobe."

The God kissed me on the lips. His breath was mingled wine and vomit, topped with a purée of peacocks' brains. "My wife," he said — and he giggled, thinking the world taken in by the deception — "my wife speaks truth indeed."

"Yes, Lucius," I said, smiling sweetly.

He whispered in my ear, "Would that *she* were as gentle, as compassionate, as you."

"I *am* that she," I said. "As you have commanded."

"You're not my mother," he said abruptly, and looked away.

I had not managed to get away with anything. But then, he said to Paris in a changed tone of voice, "You'll teach me all your techniques. Even the Pater Patriae can learn from the least of his children."

"Yes, Divinity," said Paris, bowing again.

"Be off with you. Epaphroditus will summon you for my lessons."

And Nero put his arm over my shoulder, and led me to where Tiridates was sitting. "Enjoy him," he said, and handed me over. "I mean, her." He started to giggle. Then, loud enough for the whole court to here, "Let it be known that in my magnanimity, I share with you even my very pregnant wife."

As he seemed to have made some kind of official pronouncement, the guests began to applaud. He held up his hand for silence. Then he pushed me at his guest, and wandered off, followed by Epaphroditus and assorted Praetorians.

I sat down at the Imperial triclinium, next to the Armenian King.

"This night has been something of a shambles, hasn't it?" Tiridates said, slapping a cheeky Nubian delicatus out of the way. "And I have many more days of Himself's largesse to contend with, before I make my way back to my own country and try to put it back together after a devastating war of succession."

A slave offered us kylixes of snow-cooled wine, each beautifully hand-painted and red-on-black with a scene from the amours of Jupiter. "Look," said the King. "I've got Ganymede. Who did you get?"

"Leda, I think," I said, since my cup portrayed a woman embracing a swan. "Will you take me to bed?"

"I think not," said Tiridates. "My tastes are not quite as catholic as the average Roman aristocrat. And we have more spectacle at dawn. A sea-battle in the Circus, I'm told. Salamis reenacted."

"More Aeschylus," I said. "Hoary."

Tiridates laughed. "But it will be with a touch of contemporary realism," he said, "because I'm sure we will get to see the Persians actually drown."

"We take our make-believe seriously here in Rome," I said, surprised at how much I sounded like Poppaea ... her archness, her seemingly flippant view of serious matters such as love and death ... hiding a deep vulnerability.

"Ah, Poppaea," he said softly. Perhaps he knew her. He seemed to feel for her. "I am sure you want to find out how she really is."

"You know I am not allowed to answer that."

"Let me help you," he said. "Come, I'll put my arm around you, and I'll walk you back to the palace. Everyone will make the assumption. Once you escort me to my quarters, you can slip away."

I called for Hylas to bring the cheetah. He and Simon were barely managing to restrain him, between the two of them and the golden leash.

"I'm not sure what I'm supposed to do with Hercules," I said.

"No worry, domine," Hylas said. "Slaves already tell me what to do." He had the ability of a slave to figure out exactly what to do and who was who, even though he could hardly speak Latin; this is how a slave survives.

My status, and the King's, demanded a Praetorian escort, but they discreetly left us when we reached the vestibule and turned down the corridor towards the royal guest quarters. Only my two slaves and the cheetah remained, following us at a cautious distance.

After I left Tiridates, my slaves and I went to my chambers. The boys could not easily help me undress, because Hercules was fretting. At length, I took his chain myself, and he quieted down; Hylas and Simon took off my stola and my jewelry and gave me a simple tunica, and they washed away much of the white lead makeup — it was thickly applied and would take days to remove properly — and now, I was a boy again.

I did not feel any different.

"And now," I said to Hylas, "I need to find out where the real Empress is."

"No need," Simon said. "She's in the Divinitas's bed chamber."

As I have said, slaves always know everything.

"Is she … alive?"

"For now," Simon said. "That's what Epictetus told me."

It was perhaps the only area in the palace that I was confident I could find from my own apartments. "Stay here," I said. "I'll take Hercules back to his mistress."

XVII
THE LABYRINTH OF NIGHT

A woman blocked my way.

She was slight, plainly dressed, unpainted. I could not tell if she was free or slave; that's rare. Slaves, even the wealthiest and most influential, give off certain clues. Perhaps, even, it's a smell.

She wasn't a slave, but she wasn't entirely a person, either.

She had been beautiful, still was. And she stood in the doorway of the Divinitas's as if she owned the place.

"You do look like her," she said. "At least, when you don't look too closely."

"You're not surprised to see me?"

"Here, I'll take the cheetah." Hercules went to her immediately; I had thought he would only behave this way with me. That's how I knew who she was.

"Actë," I said.

"Boy's got a brain."

She motioned me into the chamber and that's when I

saw that there was a all kinds of strangers clustered around the Divinitas's lectus. I heard someone moaning. Poppaea. She was not dead, then, though she was in pain.

To Actë I said, "I have been told that you always appear at significant moments, like a kind of death-goddess, or an angel of death. So this moment, whatever it is, is important."

She said, "The young do love to cut through to the truth," and stroked my hair. "Go and see her; she wants to see you."

She clapped her hands and all the hangers-on stepped back. I could see there were priests, slaves, a manicurist, a doctor. As I went toward the bed they were propping up Poppaea against some cushions. She was pale. Weakly she touched my arm.

I sat down beside her. She clutched my arm with surprising strength.

"Were you good?" she said softly.

"I don't think I convinced anyone for a minute," I said.

"Maybe you were there to convince only one person, not that you are me, but that he has a viable alternative. But he doesn't, you know. You will never be me."

"I never tried to be."

She had a faraway look. "You didn't play with him when he was a child. And you didn't love him before there the slightest glimmer of his becoming a God …"

"Nor did you," said Actë.

"No. That would be you," Poppaea said weakly.

"Yes. I'm the one who saw him as he was," Actë said. "I'm the one who knows the child inside the madman. But this boy … he glimpses it, too."

It was true. Actë guarded the room the way Cerberus

guards the gates of hell. She would not have let me in if she hadn't seen something in me.

In a corner of the room, a slave was casually wringing the necks of white doves and tossing them on a makeshift altar. "Poor little birdies," said the Empress. "Those sacrifices never work, anyway."

"Blasphemy!" a priest murmured.

Poppaea laughed, a dry humorless laugh.

"There seems to be a lull," she said to me. "Between bouts of agony, I'm actually able to have a conversation now. But this baby will kill me."

Another priest walked by, scattering incense.

In another corner, they were brewing a foul-smelling potion.

Poppaea reached up and gripped my arm. "Find Nero. I want Saturn to see Jupiter. A new god will slay the old. That's how the universe works. Saturn may swallow his children, but they will still cut their way out. You're the future, Sporus. Find him."

Poppaea began screaming.

***

I went out into the night. I had an idea where he might be in the lupanar, where I had last seen him go to vent his frustrations. I did not go alone, but was carried in an imperial litter and followed at a distance by some of Poppaea's men. As we turned a corner into the suburra I stopped the convoy. I got out. I explained to the henchmen that we didn't want to arouse suspicion. And Tigellinus and his gang were doubtless concealed somewhere here as well, as I understood the Emperor's night-wanderings.

Though the alley was empty, I could feel eyes everywhere. Eyes in the shadows of doorways. Eyes behind corners. Some buildings were hastily thrown up again after the fire, in a matter of days, flimsy, even taller and more precarious than before. Tiny windows had eyes as well. I could feel them.

The alley was lit only by moonlight.

I slid through a narrow door. A grating voice asked me if I was buying or selling. A torch-boy held up a candle and the burly door slave looked into my eyes.

"I want to speak to Spider," I said, popping a dupondius into his palm.

"Yes, young master," he said unctuously. "Slumming, are we?"

"Don't be impertinent," I said, using the voice one used with slaves — how easily it came to an ex-slave! — and this hulking, oiled giant let me passed and skulked into the background.

The antechamber was almost empty because the whole city was still celebrating the coronation of Tiridates. Two haggard women were kissing in one corner, and a large eunuch was wolfing down grilled pigeons in another, spitting out the bones. Spider was sitting at a table, counting stacks of spintriae, the tokens used to pay for the brothel's services. She looked up.

"Sporus," she said, and smiled. "Come sit with me. It's a slow night."

"I need to talk to Himself," I said.

"Sporus … that simply can't happen."

"Poppaea's about to give birth. She wants him to see his child. She's very … she looks *haunted,* Spider. She feels like there's a kind of doom hanging over her head."

"You can't go in, Sporus. You can't."

"Spider ... *Actë* is in the Divinitas's bedchamber."

"Ah. Like Hermes, appearing as messenger of death. Or like the Egyptians' jackal-god."

I owed Poppaea something. I had been play-acting all day, pretending to be the Empress while the real Poppaea was in labor. Himself had used me — but for what? Why was it necessary to have this charade of a ex-slave playing an Empress? What message was he sending to Tiridates — indeed to Poppaea?

The Goddess was not expendable. She'd told me so herself. I hadn't known him as a child. I didn't even know him now.

But somehow, for some reason, she wanted *me* to fetch him to her.

I was playing a role in cosmic some drama, penned by an unknown poet, a play from which I could not escape.

I knew where the secret room was ... I had been there. I had watched the two Divinities shrieking at each other like a fishwives in the forum.

I bounded up the narrow staircase. I knew where I was going. Spider was struggling to keep up. More stairs, uneven, creaky. I strode down a corridor. I threw open a door.

Himself was with a woman. That in itself was no surprise. They were going at it with enthusiasm. The room was well lit, with a row of oil lamps; their shadows thrusted and parried on the ceiling, larger than life.

At this moment, I really did not care whether I lived or died. Somehow I had to get Poppaea's message through.

"Lucius!" I shouted.

What happened next I could scarcely believe. The

Emperor had his arms around the woman and had been pulling her up and pushing her down like a toy. When he heard my voice, he let go and she tumbled to the floor. "No, no," the Emperor cried, "don't torment me, not here, not here, mother!"

He flung himself naked at the empty air.

The woman pulled a length of cloth and threw it over herself, covering herself completely except for the oval of her face. I had seen her somewhere, but I could not place her.

I realized that Spider had followed me all the way into the room.

When she saw the woman, she hissed, "Avert your eyes! Don't you know who that is?"

At that point, another door on the opposite side of the room burst open. It was Tigellinus. I did not know whether I should be glad to see him, but perhaps, at least, someone else could now take charge. "Tigellinus," I said, "the Empress asked me to find the Divinitas and let him know she is about have the child."

"Right," Tigellinus said. He seemed distracted.

More guards trooped in. They took the woman into custody.

"You're arresting her?" I said.

"The slave woman here ... was she a witness?"

I nodded.

They seized Spider as well.

"Torture?" said one of the guards.

Spider stood there, stiff, unemotional.

"Torture?" Tigellinus said offhandedly. "Of course. Make it quick, and try not to kill her."

I realized what I had done. I had sealed Spider's fate.

Slaves were not allowed to give evidence except under torture. It was an ironclad law of the Empire. Stupidly, I had nodded when they asked me if she was a witness. I looked at her. She did not seem to blame me.

"You can't torture her," I said. "I won't let you." I turned to the Divinitas. "Tell them, Divinitas. Please, I beg you."

But the Divinitas seemed to have shrunk into a mere shell of himself. He did not look at me. I wondered whether he thought that somehow I was possessed by the spirit of his mother Agrippina. The Emperor did not even seem to be in the same room as the rest of us. He did not look at me, or Spider, or Tigellinus, or the woman, who still said nothing.

Tigellinus said to me, "This time, boy, he actually can't do anything. Go with the Divinitas. Take him to Poppaea. We'll handle this."

I said, "You'll *handle* this? But he's a god! This woman, she's like a mother to me."

"Not a very auspicious thing to be saying to the Divinitas," Tigellinus said, cracking a smile. "He didn't exactly have a good relationship with *his* mother."

"He doesn't understand," said Spider. "Let's get this over with."

"What do you mean?" I said. "Nero Claudius Caesar Augustus Germanicus is God! There's no one he can't have. He owns every one of us. What is so different about this woman?"

At last, the woman spoke. The room fell silent. "My name is Rubria," she said. "I am a Vestal Virgin."

XVIII

THE TRIAL OF THE VESTAL

You actually witnessed it? The notorious defilement of Rome's very essence? The God of Rome descending to the most depraved befouling of Rome?

Yes. But I did not really understand what it was I had seen. I thought I had seen everything. He had defiled prostitutes and married women, men and women, and even allowed himself to be used as a pathicus. I know that to a Roman male, to be so used was as low as you could go. I did not know then that this was an order of baseness far beyond the shame of allowing Himself to be penetrated by a lowly slave like me.

But you know now. The Vestals guard the flame. The flame is Rome. Without the flame, Rome perishes. Nothing else is as important.

I had thought that Nero was Rome. But there's only been an Emperor for a hundred years. And we're past the Eighth Century of the the city's foundation. And all that time, the Vestals have tended the sacred flame.

You were told these things when you were brought here. You had a tutor who taught you well.

As I stood there, I remembered some of the history Aristarchos had taught me. I remembered, then, the Vestals' seats in the circus, the only seats that afforded as fine a view as the Emperor's box. Though I was not Roman, I knew the Vestals were untouchable; they were the city's living symbol, keeping the flame alive at the oldest temple in Rome, a flame which had not been doused in eight hundred years.

That infamy alone would have been enough for the Emperor to be declared damnatio memoriae, *and all mentions of Himself removed from history.*

And yet, to my still uneducated mind, she was still just some woman I had stumbled on *in flagrante* with Himself, not an unusual thing. And for some unfathomable reason, they were taking Spider, whom I loved, off to be tortured, and my master, the Owner of the World, was not lifting a finger to prevent it.

But now, I suppose you know what they had to do to Rubria.

Yes. And I know why Nero could do nothing.

***

The Emperor left by a secret stairway, and out a hidden doorway. He insisted that I follow him. He kept me close, clutching my arm at times. Some Praetorians followed at a distance. I was not able to see them take away the Vestal Virgin, or my friend who I was powerless to save.

A litter, unadorned, carried by a gang of mismatched slaves, stood in wait. A slave stepped out and crouched so the Emperor could step in. He dragged me up as well. The slave had not seen this coming and had started to scurry away, so I hit my head on one of the supports. Nero was so distracted he did not even order a whipping.

We moved quickly; the litterbearers may not have been a matched set, but they were quick and smooth. Inside, it was dark, and dank from the Emperor's sweat. As we sped along, one of the attendants pushed a lit lychnus through the curtain; I took it. It was one of those erotic terracotta lamps; I had seen them in the brothel; it was made in the shape of a rampant satyr, with the wick protruding from the creature's prodigious member. In the flickering light I saw that the master of the world was hunched at the farthest corner of the litter, and he seemed defeated, helpless.

Softly, I said, "Poppaea asked for you, demanded that I fetch you."

"She will have to wait."

"She's in labour and having a hard time of it."

"Impossible! She's a goddess!" But his tone was unconvincing; it was, almost, imploring.

"Perhaps," I said, trying a fresh approach, "as a goddess, she feels no pain, but here, living amongst men, she feigns her suffering out of consideration for the humans who surround her... surely *you've* done things like that, Divinitas. Or people would be ..."

"Blinded," he whispered. "Yes, blinded by my true form. As when Semele gazed on Jupiter."

"There, there," I said, and with my free hand I stroked his arm.

"My mother never accepted that of me," he said.

The God was no different from Poppaea's cheetah, after all. He just needed a little empathy.

"Shall we go to Poppaea now?" I said at last.

"Not just yet. We have one stop to make."

Indeed, I could sense that we were not going uphill,

toward the summit of the Capitoline.

***

At length, the litter stopped. The curtains were drawn and the crouching slave returned. I stepped out first and helped Himself the Divine Nero down.

"Wine," he said.

Magically, it seemed, an exquisite kylix of snow-cooled wine was proffered out of the gloomy. Torches were being lit. We were in a garden. Next to the pathway, there was a row of statues. all stately women, decorously clad, their stolas reaching down past their toes. Their faces, discreetly painted, stared down at us like an army of avenging furies.

The pathway we stood on led to a portico, a columned façade, a huge door. The door swung open and first there came women bearing a gilded curule, which they unfolded and set down just behind the top stair. Himself, leaning on me, made his way to the seat of office and sat down.

Then about six women and some attendants emerged, the last a withered crone who nevertheless moved with the energy of a teenaged girl. She spoke to the Emperor in a sharp voice, utterly disregarding his Divine status. She and the others wore the snow-white palla and covered their heads with a purple-bordered white suffibulum.

"A fine mess you've made of things, Lucius Domitius!"

"I'm sorry, Great-Aunt," said the Emperor meekly.

The Senior Vestal must have been some neglected member of a family connected to the Julio-Claudians in some way. Perhaps they'd all had to commit suicide in some earlier purge, with the matron left to rot as the most exalted female in the Empire.

"Very well," she said. "Let's get this over with."

The Emperor summoned me and I sat at his feet. So I saw all of it. Tigellinus brought in Rubria. She was not restrained in any way, but left to walk by herself, with a quiet dignity.

Then Spider was dragged in. To say she had been tortured does not begin to describe the wreck she had become. I saw, too, that her fingers had been smashed. Her clothing was bloody. Yet when she looked at me, I saw no resentment. She knew there was nothing I could have done, once she had followed me up those steps.

Tigellinus said, "Did you see this woman in the act of sexual congress with a man?"

"Yes," Spider said.

I whispered in the Emperor's ear. "Please, Lucius. Give her to me. Her fingers are broken. She can no longer perform her work. What good is to anyone?"

"Oh, you and your delicate heart, Sporus! I was just going to have her crucified, expunge this whole sordid incident from the universe."

I kissed his hands. He seemed immovable. How could I save the woman I'd unthinkingly condemned to such suffering. "My Lord, my Divinitas, my Love," I said. "Just give me this little thing and I'll ..." But I could not think of what act I could perform that he could not demand at any time.

I thought back to my training, when I was in the slaves' holding area in Ostia. All those lists of self-debasements that I had been fortunate to avoid because my master was Petronius. Something sprang to my lips. "Please, tata," I said, and almost meant it.

The master of the world held me to his bosom. He held me so tightly I thought I would suffocate. His sadness found a strange echo in my own. I remembered that the Divinitas's real father had died when he was two, and that the Divine Claudius had adopted him as his heir when he was thirteen, and only at the machinations of his mother Agrippina; I doubted he had called Claudius *tata* either. Letting myself be enfolded in him, I found I could not summon up any image of my own father in my mind.

"All right," he said. "Tigellinus, have the slave sent to —"

"Petronius's villa," I said. Surely Croesus would know how to bring her back from the infernum I had cast her into.

"Touching," said the Maxima Vestalis, "though hardly relevant to the business at hand. You must pronounce sentence, Lucius Domitius."

"I?" said the Divinitas. "But … the sentence is already known."

"But only you can utter it. You are the Pontifex Maximus, the upholder of the state religion."

"Must I? It's not as if I *enjoy* killing people."

"Well then," said Rubria, "while you're dithering around, I want to speak." No one stopped her. "I was six years old when I was pledged here. I was told that I would be one of the most sacred persons in the world. That all would respect me and know that by tending the fire, I keep the Empire alive. But you will never know how wretched a time I've had. Your great-auntie is a petty scold who belittles us and metes out oppressive punishments for silly infractions. Oh, you haven't tied your ribbons right. There's a corner of the hearth unswept. A whipping without any dinner. My parents bought political favour with my soul, and then your mother made them commit suicide anyway. There's nothing for me here, do you understand?" She walked right up to Himself and spoke directly in his face. "Then *you* came. You sang songs. You made beautiful poetry. You smelled like the spring. You told me I wasn't breaking my vows, because you were not a man. You were a God! How was I to know? Had I ever had a man? Did I know what it is men and women do? Of course not. You taught me. The House of the Vestals is death, worse than death. You awakened me out of the cold ground. Put me back there, at least I've lived."

The Vestals shrieked and made all sorts of gestures of averting every possible omen, tearing at their veils, uttering ritual formulae, beating their breasts. Amid the cacophony, Nero found his voice. Still clutching me to his breast, he said, "There is only one punishment for *incestum* committed by a Vestal Virgin. To lay a hand on you, to shed your blood, is anathema, and therefore your death must be entirely free of bloodletting. You must therefore, without coercion, of your own free will, be buried alive in the Campus Sceleratus. Let it happen *now*, under cover of night, while the city is preoccupied with celebrating the coronation of Tiridates."

So saying, he got up, letting go of me so suddenly that I tripped on the stairs. He marched toward his litter and I followed.

When we were moving again, he said, "No, don't ask me. We are not going back to the palace yet. We will see this story through to its end."

I only started to say the name "Poppaea" when he stopped my lips with ... perhaps it was a kiss. Perhaps it was the hungry bite of a ravening beast. I dared not pull away, until he did, abruptly. Not a moment too soon, because his cloak had almost caught fire on the lamp I had stupidly been clutching in one hand.

"Poppaea sent you, didn't she?"

I did not answer, because he knew the answer.

"She sent you so that I would *have* to kill her. I never want to kill anyone. Not even those benighted Chrestianoi. Let alone my mother. Poppaea is playing a game and she has forgotten that she only wins when I let her."

I thought of the Lady Poppaea Sabina, whose friendship — or manipulative scheming — had brought me to this moment. I thought of her, surrounded by people in the imperial bedchamber, surrounded yet friendless.

"I will never play games with you, My Lord," I said … playing the ultimate game … "I love you."

I did not ask him to love me. That was not my place. I could not ask. I dared not. For to be loved by Nero was a death warrant.

XIX

CAMPUS SCELERATUS

Nothing they do to me today will be as horrific as what they did to Rubria. They managed to pull together a funeral procession with twenty pairs of torchbearers, and we proceeded toward the Colline Gate with drums, double-flutes, and sobbing professional mourners.

It had been less than a day and a night, and I had already been present at a coronation in the forum, Greek drama, gladiatorial combats, a lavish banquet, a flirtation by a king, the bedside of a childbirth, a sacrilegious act of incestum, and a trial.

The funeral had been put together at, it seemed, a moment's notice, but Rubria played her part as though she had rehearsed for it, walking with dignity in the procession towards her own execution.

When we arrived at the Field of Evil, the soldiers had

everything ready. They must have been digging all through the trial, because the pit was already prepared. It was surrounded on three sides by torch-bearers. It was not wide — the slave quarters I shared with Hylas and Hyacinth in the bowels of Petronius's villa was no wider.

Himself's curule was set up at the very edge of the pit, and I stood beside him. I was able to see clearly, then, Rubria's journey to infernum, which was by way of a rickety wooden ladder, accompanied by a priest, who then abandoned her and pulled up the ladder. Below, we could see, she had a couch to sit in, what looked like a jug of wine, some bread, some olives.

She sat completely unmoved. And Himself did not look down at her at all.

It was when they slammed down the lid of her burial chamber that the screaming began. Undeterred, the soldiers began to shovel earth back into the pit. The screaming was terrible to hear but it grew faint as the opening was filled. No one made a sound. Just the sound of earth piling up, and the slowly fading screams. The softer the screams, the more bloodcurdling. Presently they seemed no more than the squeak of a mouse in a jar in the kitchen, and yet — in that deafening silence — the sounds were stab-wounds to the soul.

The soldiers began to pat down the earth. Soon we would see only level ground. We could walk over her as she ran out of air. She would always be with us, living, even in death.

Himself the Divinitas called for his lyre. He held it in one arm, with the other poised to begin some epic threnody. But no words came.

Instead of an Imperial dirge, there came a chill wind,

unseasonal. The wind whispered and sighed and I fancied I could still hear the Vestal Virgin's cries.

Nero did not move.

At length, Tigellinus approached him and said, in a surprisingly solicitous tone, "We should get going, Divinitas. You haven't slept for more than a day and a night."

"And well you shouldn't," said the Vestalis Maxima, not giving the god any quarter. "Take the boy and go to bed."

"Yes, Great-Aunt," said Himself, barely audible.

The withered chief vestal leaned over and presented her cheek for Himself to kiss. He did so, dutifully.

Then I helped him into his litter, and we began the procession back to the palace.

#

"No light," he said, as I held up the little erotic lamp. "I want to sit in the dark."

And so we did.

The way back was mostly uphill, and the bearers had been standing at attention for hours and were doubtless exhausted; it was a slow journey back.

"I know what you want to say," said the Emperor.

Which was strange, for I did not know it myself.

In the utter dark, in the oppressive closeness of the closed litter, in the sweltering stillness that fell as soon as the curtain shut out the wind, I felt I could say anything. "What do I want to say?" I asked Himself, not even addressing him by any title. Like an equal.

"You want to say I should have done something."

I did not answer.

"Admit it. Should have, would have, ought to have … wherever I step, the path branches a millionfold, and I always step wrong. I could never do anything right. I've always known. Agrippina told me often enough."

I let him speak.

"How old were you when they ripped you from everything you knew?"

"Where I lived, Divinitas, they didn't really number the years. Only if someone grew big enough to do a man's work."

"When I was two, my father died. I went to the country. I lived what some might call … a normal life. I played music. I read poets. I even farmed. I grew up with, I was in love with, a slave girl, I was with her all the time, in my loneliness, she saw me; in her alienation, I saw her."

I do not know whether Himself had singled me out to be the one he should open up to, or whether, in the darkness, he saw no one at all, and felt himself alone; I had been a slave, I knew that they are often invisible; that is why they know everything.

"You mean Actë," I said. "Tell me about Actë, my Lord."

"What's to tell? She played no games."

"I know." More than any other woman of the court, Actë had seen through all my attempts to shield my soul.

"You know?"

"I saw her," I said. "I told you. She's with the Empress right now, guarding her while she's in labour."

"It's bad, then," he said. "She only comes at the turning points."

The litter turned uphill; I could not keep my balance at the steep angle and slid into the Emperor's arms. Startled, I cried out. He held me as a child holds a doll. Through the perfume, I smelled stale sweat, sour wine, and a tinge of vomit. I did not struggle, did not try to wrest myself free; the incline of the street pushed me more tightly against him.

"Call me tata again," said the master of the world.

"Tata."

He turned me around and kissed me. I tasted his tears.

"I'm not evil," he said.

"No," I said. "You're a god. You're like the wind, like the sea."

"Yes. I can't help killing people. I bear them no malice."

He squeezed me so tightly that I thought I too would be killed that night. I knew he could feel my pounding heart. He must know, I thought, the stark terror inside me, even though I am doing everything I can to appear unmoved.

I closed my eyes.

In my memory, I smelled the sea. The salt tang of captivity.

"You too are a slave," I said softly.

I did nothing. I exercised none of the arts I had been trained in. I leaned against a cushion and became almost a boy-shaped cushion myself, allowing him to do as he pleased, giving nothing in return. I will not feel anything, I told myself sternly, remembering the salted, decapitated head of the Lady Claudia Octavia, remembering the broken body of my friend Spider, remembering the haughty demeanour of the Virgo Vestalis Rubria as she descended into the abyss, and the faint screams that echoed up from the freshly-shovelled earth. I will feel *nothing,* I told myself. It was still pitch dark. We were still moving uphill.

And yet … in the end, as he flailed in the ocean of his passion, clinging to me as though to the broken beam of a wrecked shipping floating on the waves, I did feel the ghost of a feeling. Or was it just my young body, responding instinctively to being touched?

"Tata," I whimpered, clawing at him a little.

And immediately, the master of the world shuddered, exploded, and was still.

The incline levelled off. I was jerked upright and Himself slid off me. We were both slippery. The litter came to a stop.

I reached outside with the unlit lamp, and pulled it back in, lit. I saw the face of the Divinitas. Not a trace of that vulnerability I had felt when we were cocooned in the pitch black of the closed litter. He glanced at me, holding up the lamp, and might as well have been a piece of furniture, a lamp-stand carved into the shape of a Ganymede.

So quietly that I barely heard him, he said, "I suppose I shall have to go and kill my wife now."

XX

IMPERATRIX

Yes, I saw Nero kill his wife.

With your own eyes.

Yes.

It's all true, then.

But not the way they told it, and not the way it will be told. Because the world is always more complex than the words of any historian.

***

The Emperor walked purposefully, grimly, not speaking; I followed. He took a back corridor and a flight of steps I had never taken before; almost by magic, we arrived at the Imperial apartments.

And Actë was still the gatekeeper; in all that time, she seemed not to have moved. But she *knew.* And Nero avoided her gaze. He knew that she knew. He looked at the floor, like a chidden boy.

There were fewer people in the room now. The air was still cloudy with incense, but the priests, doctors, soothsayers and hangers-on had mostly cleared the room. There was a midwife and a few other female slaves; they clustered at one end of the lectus. There were no baby cries. Perhaps it had not yet come.

Poppaea was no longer screaming. At first I thought she must be dead, but then I heard whimpers. One of the women came up to me and told me she was asking for me. The Divinitas was still shrinking from Actë's baleful gaze. I left him there and went to the Empress's bedside.

The cheetah lay next to her on the lectus. The pungent feline smell mingled with the stench of the unguents and the blood, and the perfumes that had been used to mask the odors, and the sick-sweet smell of the frankincense.

I sat down. She touched my arm.

"My twin sister," she said. Her voice was weak, but her mind was not clouded.

I kissed her on the cheek.

She said to me, "You were my secret weapon, Sporus."

"So you told me."

"I never realized I would turn the weapon on myself, little brother."

"You just said I was your twin sister," I said.

She smiled. "As my sister, we're of an age, but as my brother, you're just a chid."

I managed a kind of laugh, because she obviously did not want me to seem too sad. "You see," she went on, "how Actë handles him. No one else can."

"Why isn't *she* the Empress then?"

"She has no aristocratic blood at all. In fact, she's an ex-slave."

"I am, too," I said. "Which means he can never …" It was unthinkable in any case.

"But you're a prince," she said softly.

"I was told to say so," I said, "so they'd pay more for me at the auction."

"Oh, Sporus, Sporus," she said. "It's your innocence that appeals to him the most, you know. To all of us. Petronius, too. You're like a marble statue that has just come from the sculptor's studio — all white, all featureless. And in that whiteness, every colour is possible. And then, on the way to the temple, or to the public square, the painters come, and the statue becomes just a single someone. But before that … Sporus, in you, we all see the persons we want to see. But only you know the person you are."

"I just play whatever role I have to," I said, "to survive through to the next day."

"You must. But, Sporus, don't dishonour my name," said the Empress. And turned the other cheek for me to kiss.

"No," I said, not knowing if it was a promise I could keep.

The midwife interrupted. "Augusta," she said, "will you look at the child?"

"No," said the Lady Poppaea Sabina, mistress of the world.

But I saw the baby. A wet-nurse held him, was feeding him. He made no sound. "Is he well?" I said.

"Barely clinging to life," said the midwife.

"Sporus," Poppaea said, "stay in the shadows for a little while."

I kissed her cheek again. Then I slipped to the far side of

the room. I was about to witness a ceremony that takes place in every Roman home when a child is born. A chair was brought for Himself. He sat down, still not looking at his wife.

The wet-nurse came forward and laid the child at the Emperor's feet.

He scrutinized the baby for a long while.

The baby sneezed. Spluttered a little, then was silent again. Not dead, but, as Poppaea had said, clinging to life.

Any moment now, I thought, the Divinitas will pick up the child. It is the absolute right of the paterfamilias in any Roman household to determine whether a child should be accepted or rejected. The baby is laid on the ground, and the paterfamilias picks it up. If he does not, the baby is taken outside and exposed. In the country, it is probably wolves; in the city, most likely, a passing slaver looking for a quick profit.

"Do you think he looks like me?" said Himself.

No one answered.

"Actë, tell me," he said.

She turned her back on him; even I knew how unspeakably rude that was.

"Sporus," he said. "Come here."

I was reluctant to, but I did not have the kind of self-confidence that the Lady Actë displayed. Making as little noise as possible, I crept up and crouched at the foot of the Divinitas's sella.

"He looks like the Empress, doesn't he?"

"Very much so," I said.

The Emperor was looking from the child to me, and not to Poppaea lying on the bed. First me, then the child, the child, then me. "Those pouting lips," he said. He put a stubby finger on my mouth. It tasted sweaty, and oily, and a little bit of semen, as well; the episode in the litter was still fresh. "But tell me, my dearest," he went on, "shouldn't the child also look like *me?*"

He ran his finger down my chin, to the nape of my neck, to my shoulder. I must say that it made my flesh crawl. But I remained numb, showing no emotion.

"Whose is it?" Nero said softly.

Poppaea said, almost inaudibly, "You know, Lucius."

"Lucius!" the Emperor screamed.

"Why Lucius," she said. "Lucius … Domitius … Ahenobarbus, called Nero." She only spoke in gasps.

"How many men are there named Lucius?" said Nero. "There are only a dozen praenomina in all of the Empire! Shall I crucify one in twelve of all the citizens of Rome?"

"Don't be absurd, Lucius," she said.

"You don't think I remember the day I wanted you to come to the theatre, and you begged off because of a headache? Whose bed did you climb into that night?"

"That was months ago."

"Exactly! *Nine* months."

He had been nursing this imagined slight for almost a year, and it had grown into something monstrous.

"Adulteress!" he screamed

That was when the kicking began. I had seen him do this before. I had not understood until today that their relationship had deteriorated into nothing but violence. I did not look after the first kick. I squeezed my eyes tight shut. I hoped, I prayed that the first had been enough. Finally, when I summoned up the will to open my eyes, I could see that she lay quite still, and there was blood everywhere.

I was beyond terror. Inside, I was cold and dead.

There was no honour, no beauty. Petronius's death had had a kind of nobility. Even Rubria's cruel punishment had a kind of ceremonial gravitas that made it almost bearable. This was unremitting savagery. I understood for the first time why the Chrestianoi called him *The Beast*.

They took her away, then. The slaves, the soldiers, their faces frozen into masks of unfeeling. The room began to empty.

Himself, the Divinitas, sat at the edge of the lectus. Two slaves, the few who remained with us, began to undress him, with swift, practiced movements, making themselves as invisible as possible.

I had not been dismissed.

"You see how it is," said Nero. "I can't love women. When I do, I kill them." He was not speaking to me. I realized that Actë was still there, standing behind me; she had not looked away.

She said, "Your problem, Lucius, is that in the end, all women, to you, are just your mother."

"^*You're* not," said the Emperor.

"But you know why I can't be an Empress," she said.

"Yes. Agrippina won't let you."

"But she's dead," I said.

Actë turned to me. "How little you know, little boy. Agrippina will never die. He will kill her again and again, and she will still haunt him."

Nero wept.

"Better you take the boy," said Actë. "You won't have to kill him. Agrippina will understand there's nothing to worked up about. It's only a boy."

"Even *she* can't be Empress," I began ... "Well, I'm not

even a woman."

"No," said Nero. "But then again, I am a God. That which mortals but dream, I can make real. My word alone makes flesh out of the empty air."

Actë said, "I love you. You are everything to me. I live only for you. And yet I know that you are mad."

And she left the room.

The Emperor said nothing more that night. He reached for my hand and drew me to the bed with an unexpected gentleness. He kissed my hands. I think he was trying to apologise, although I was not the one he had wronged. And all night long, he stroked and kissed me, his tenderness surpassed only by my terror.

The child remained on the floor.

XXI

THE MORNING AFTER THE NIGHT BEFORE

And this was how the morning after was: I woke up alone.

The child had been discreetly removed, and from then on it was as if it had never drawn breath.

Sunlight streamed in from an entryway that led to a private garden I had never seen.

I woke alone and despite the light, this might as well have been deepest Tartarus.

I did not want to remember the night. We had made love. Well, the Divinitas had made love, while I, like a doll, was but the empty vessel of his imagination.

In time I must have passed out, but my dreams were if anything more unnerving that what had happened in that endless day and night that had transpired. For a time, I remember, I floated.

A pendulum swung back and forth. No, not a pendulum, but a bottle in a cave, strung up be a hemp cord, and inside it a lone cricket stridulated. I knew this place; it was the dwelling the of Sybil, who knew all the world's secrets, and who was cursed with immortality. In the dream I wandered from cave to cave. Those I encountered looked away, as though seeing me was unbearable.

I understood then; they were the dead. They did not like to see a living person. Perhaps I reminded them of when they had been alive. They were shadowlike, translucent. It was a labyrinth, but the walls themselves moved and shifted, and wherever I went, I found I had gone nowhere. And then, without warning, I found myself at the foot of a mountain of potshards and rubbish. In my dream, I had reached Mount Testaceus, where the refuse of the city was piled up, where my friend Hyacinth still lay, I supposed. For he too had been added to the refuse that the city regurgitated every day, the mountain of the unwanted.

My dream had brought me here for a reason. Hyacinth's shade was reaching out to me.

No sooner had I realized this than he was there. He was embracing me. It was as though he were still alive. I felt him, I smelled him, I looked into his eyes and saw the longing that had led him to walk this path.

He's with me not in memory but in an eternal present.

Sporus. He doesn't call me Sporus but a secret name, in our own tongue. I cannot utter this name he calls me by, because you don't know our language. In our world, true names are secrets shared only among the most intimate.

We commune with mind alone. *How is it that I can feel you, that you don't seem dead at all?*

I am just a shadow.

But I feel you! I hear your blood racing, your heart beating when you put your arms around me!

It's the echo of your own heart. It's the rushing of the blood in your own veins. I only live because you live. When you stop living, we'll be shadows together.

Petronius once quoted Euripides to me: *Kai pos an autos katthanoi te kai blepoi? …* "how can you be both dead and alive?" … Hyacinth reads my thoughts and answers, *I don't know. I only know you're here and that makes me be here as well. Is Hylas looking after you?*

As far as he can.

He is a little out of his depth.

I am having this dream, I told myself, because there's something I need to know. Something is going to happen.

In my dream Hyacinth hugs me so hard he's almost *inside* me. And he says, *Sporus, Sporus, let me live through you, let me have the life that the knife took from me.*

The memory of the dream faded, and once more I was in the Imperial cubiculum. I did not know if I had leave to return to my quarters, or to go back to Petronius's house, which was the one place I could think of as home. I did not know if the Emperor had

I was hungry. There was not a single slave in shouting distance. I could not even see a convenient urine jar.

It would not hurt to go into the garden, surely. So, still bleary-eyed, I stepped into the bright sunlight.

This was a simpler garden than the ones I had seen in the palace. Unlike most gardens it was not in the style of an atrium; it could be accessed only from this private cubiculum, and a wall went round it, too tall to see over. Nor could I see any part of the Palatine, looming above the wall, so the garden must be strategically placed, and near the summit of the hill.

It looked to be around the sixth hour. The sun was

directly overhead. I stood naked and alone. Presently I found what seemed to be a remote corner. It was behind a statue of Augustus. There were some rose bushes and, unable to hold it in any longer, I emptied my bladder.

I became aware of a fierce odor and when I looked down, Hercules was crouched at my feet. He was gnawing on a human hand.

"Leftovers," said the Emperor.

I turned and there he was, dwarfed by Augustus Caesar. Ruefully, he smiled. "I've been meaning to swap out the head," he said. "But if you keep pissing in the garden —"

"Divinity!" I exclaimed, and started to prostrate myself.

"Next time," he said, "just call one of your slaves."

"I don't know who my slaves are," I said.

"They're everywhere. Just say 'pisspot' very quietly, and one will appear. But the treasury loses money if we don't collect every drop."

"Why don't you tax it?" I said.

He put his arm around my bare shoulders and started to walk me back to the cubiculum. "That," he said, "is a *good* idea. Rome can't survive without clean togas, and laundries can't bleach without piss. You were always a shrewd one, Poppaea."

I did not contradict him.

"Tigellinus," he said.

By magic, the head of the Praetorians appeared, perhaps from behind a tree. One moment he was just there, as if he had *always* been there.

"Tigellinus," said Himself, "let's have a urine tax."

"It won't be popular," Tigellinus said.

"But we could finally afford to replace the remaining imperial heads."

"There might be other needs," said Tigellinus. "Judaea has revolted again." He then told the Emperor a lengthy story of how Gallus, the Imperial Legate in the province of Syria, had been ambushed by rebellious Jews.

"Send Vespasian," said Nero, and immediately changed the subject back to the urine tax.

It occurred to me that I had never been alone. All that lolling about bemoaning my aloneness in the cubiculum … who knows how many slaves there were, keeping themselves invisible until the God wanted something. Under the bed, behind a curtain, in secret compartments in the walls … no. I was never going to be alone, *ever,* as long as lived in the sphere of the Divinitas.

"Divinitas," I said softly.

"Call me Lucius."

I did not dare, not directly, not in front of Tigellinus, who saw this whole charade for what it was.

"May I have leave to visit the house of Petronius, and to see a few friends from my … former life?"

"Why are you asking?" said Tigellinus. "You are the Emperor's favorite. You can go anywhere you want, visit anyone, buy anything from the market, clothes, slaves — they will send a bill to Epaphroditus, you can be sure — and if the Divinitas needs any of your special talents, I will find you within the hour — the whole city is caught in my net."

The Emperor said, "He will need an escort. Tell Vinicius to make the boy his special duty. He is reliable, and he doesn't like boys, so he won't be tempted to touch what is mine."

What is mine.

Chilling words to hear, for one who had already been set

free.

***

But before I could leave the palace, the Divinity had need of what Tigellinus had called my "special talents" once again.

And again, I was surprised by his tenderness, his consideration. I tried to mask my terror, as much as I could. At one point, he made me cry out, and it might even have been pleasure, a momentary joy that breached an ocean of pain.

When I cried out, he stopped. He held me. He looked into my eyes with wonderment, and, quoting Virgil, said, *"Nunc scio, quid sit amor."*

"Now I know what love is," I repeated in Greek.

Perhaps he knew; I was more unsure than ever.

Then, he said the words that instantly made me understand why the ghost of Hyacinth had visited my dreams.

"Your voice is changing," he said.

XXII

Apollo Palatinus

How to avoid being hacked up and served to the Divinitas on a platter, minus my masculine parts? Because that was the unspoken menace behind the words, "Your voice is changing."

What would be better? To survive the operation, or to wander forever in shadow, like Hyacinth?

Himself left me on the bed. No sooner had he left the room than slaves came. An old man came with a wet rag, to wipe me off. A rather dour-looking woman who started to dress me without my consent, and a pretty young one with a krater of undiluted wine.

I said, "I want my own slave."

And at that moment, Hylas emerged from a secret panel in the wall.

"Me wait so long for you to call for me, domine!" he said, hugging me.

"Not me, Hylas," I said softly, "I."

"Beat me!" he said, smiling. The others looked disapproving.

"Where are the others?" I said.

Simon crawled from under the bed. "I could barely breathe," he said, "the way the Divinitas was bouncing all over you. Do you need a poultice, a salve?"

"Take me to my own quarters," I said, as I was sure I did not know the way.

I had stopped the Imperial slave from finishing dressing me, and was wearing only a simple tunica, having left my queenly robes lying in heaps. Simon and Hylas gathered those heavy garments up, then took me down passages with stairs to my apartments. I was sure I had not come the same way. I wondered if I would ever be able to find my way, and I wondered at how my slaves had already figured it all out.

I decided that I could take literally what Tigellinus had told me: that I actually had the freedom of the city, and could go where I chose, since the Praetorians evidently had eyes on every street corner and I could never be beyond the Emperor's reach. So I decided it was time to go home — Petronius's, that is.

Once there, I could confide my fears to the only people who could really understand my predicament: Croesus, Spider, and Marcus Vinicius.

***

Just as in my former life as a slave, I sat in the kitchens gossiping. I did not feel so constrained in the kitchens. Spider was a shell, an empty old woman, yet she had made some progress to returning to health. With her broken hands, she resembled her name more than before.

Croesus, free, had cast off the sense of servitude completely.

Some of the slaves were a little cautious, but when Croesus and Spider made much of me, they seemed to accept me. Though Hylas could not help calling me *master,* or pouring me a cup of humble posca from an earthenware jug.

Simon, it seemed, was a lot more impertinent. He neither called me *domine,* nor did he defer to Hylas, to whom I had given him as a tutor. Then again, he had not been born a slave.

I said, "Simon, you said you'd lace my caligae and suck my mentula."

"When do I begin?"

"But you haven't even started on the job I've given you, which is to scrub the barbarity from Hylas's lips."

"Yes, Hylas," he said. "Come on, now. *Dominus, domine, dominum, domini, domino…"*

"Why so many?" Hylas said.

"Oh, there's more," Simon said.

"All of you," I said, "leave me, because I need to have a serious discussion with people who actually understand the world."

And the slaves scattered like chaff, knowing there was an unseen boundary behind which I would never again be one of them.

I unburdened myself to Croesus, Spider, and Marcus Vinicius, telling them everything that had transpired that night, including my dream, and the words that the Divinitas spoke to me.

Marcus Vinicius said, "Could the Divinitas have spoken in jest, or just in passing?"

Spider said, "Not when you remember the dream."

"There's truth in dreams," Croesus agreed.

"Shall I wait for Hyacinth to come in another dream," I said, despairing, "before I know what to do?" For dreams come unbidden. They don't give answers on demand. Unless…

Marcus said, "You should talk to the gods."

"But which god?" Croesus said.

"I slept with one all night," I said, "and all I got was more confusion."

Spider said, "Apollo is the god who always speaks the truth."

I knew that if I went to a temple to make sacrifice or give thanks, Tigellinus's spies would think nothing of it.

"But the Temple of Apollo Palatinus was damaged in the fire," I said.

"Damaged," said Vinicius, "but still in operation."

"It is still Apollo's house," Spider said. "There are still priests, and people still go there. To speak of dreams, go in the full moon. Diana, the sun's sister, rules the night."

***

I waited until the eleventh hour. I did not want to make a big spectacle of going to the temple. I did not take Hylas, which made him pout a little, but I knew Simon could retain more of what was said. I took the second-best litter and Marcus rode alongside.

The moon had already risen. Because of the collapse of the roof during the fire, Apollo stood in the open, in the moonlight; rain and fire had worn the paint and you could see a lot of the marble. But rather than looking damaged, it seemed that you could apprehend the god's true essence beneath the paint. The god's face was ash-white in the moonlight, like a ghost. There were traces of gold. The god's eyes seemed alive. Without a roof, the clouds of incense were attenuated, the odor faint. Laurel trees stood, some intact, some partly uprooted. There was a vendor table with caged doves for sacrifice.

I sent Simon over to buy a brace of doves. I did not say they should send the bill to the palace, but when he came and told me the cheapest pair was two hundred sesterces, and that a beautiful, unblemished pair could be as much as a thousand, I realized I should have brought more than a few coins with me.

"I didn't know doves cost that much," I said to Vinicius.

"It's a temple," he said.

I wasn't sure how one could go about sending a bill to the palace, or indeed whether I really could do that. But as I was wondering what to do next, a woman swept up the steps and approached the vendor.

"A pair of the best whites," she said.

A steward, hovering behind her, counted out ten aurei. The seller took them out of the cage. The woman waved at me.

"There you go," she said. "Remember me to the Emperor."

"But—" I began.

"Who does not recognize the Divinitas's beautiful new plaything?" she said. "Put in a good word, Sporus. I had a dream last night. Meeting you here is another augury."

I looked at her in bewilderment. She was beautiful. She was nothing like Poppaea, but she carried herself the same way. Unlike the late Empress, she had not bleached her hair to match the whores of the suburra. Like Poppaea, though, she had a penetrating gaze, and her eyes, enhanced with kohl, made it hard to look away.

"What shall I say to the Divinitas?" I said.

"What you like," she said. "But let him know I exist."

She then turned back and purchased a whole cage full, and marched up the steps towards Apollo.

The vendor's boy came up to me. "Shall I wring their necks for you, sir?" he said in a piping voice. "Some of our suppliants are queasy."

"I'll kill them," Simon said. "I'm quick and they won't feel anything." To me, he added, "My people sacrifice doves as expiation, and my father always had something to feel guilty about."

I watched the lady as she prayed to Apollo Palatinus. I could not take my eyes off her, in fact. She stood there — I could not hear what she said, but she railed, she gesticulated, she *demanded* something of the god. Presently, she turned to her steward, and he opened the cage and released all the doves she had just paid a fortune for.

"Patricians! Such idiots!" said Simon. "They'll just catch them all and resell them."

The woman came charging down the steps, the steward scrambling to keep up, and I saw now that her litter was waiting at a bend in the road.

"Who is she?" I said.

"That," said Marcus Vinicius, "is the Lady Statilia Messalina, wife of the ex-consul, Marcus Julius Vestinus Atticus."

"So," the vendor's boy said, "what will it be tonight? Unlucky in love? Harm to an enemy? Dream divination?"

"Divination," Simon said, impertinent again.

Just for the sake of form, I slapped him.

"You're a slave," I said. "By the pudenda of Venus, act like one."

"Yes, domine," he said, giggling.

Vinicius said, "Sporus, this really won't do. Croesus will give him ten lashes when we get home. It's not serious, but the boy has to learn to behave properly in public."

Simon immediately became more subdued. I felt a twinge of guilt, but I didn't feel like contradicting Marcus. After all, any Roman paterfamilias would beat their own sons far more savagely, and Simon's own father had thought nothing of selling him off.

"Tell me, Marcus, what I am supposed to do," I said.

"Speak to the god," he said. "Make sure you say your name clearly; they get confused. Then ask the favor, and offer the lives of the doves. At that point Simon can wring their necks, if you don't want to."

I approached the god.

I breathed in the faint odor of incense. I bathed in the moonlight. The eyes of the god were on me.

I said, "My name is Gaius Petronius Gaii Libertus Sporus. I am other people's creation. I'm a peasant in a remote country. I'm a slave boy whose sole existence is in others' pleasure. I'm a prince who was captured by pirates. I'm Giton, the perfect boy, stepped out of the pages of Petronius's imagination. And now, it seems, they want me to be an Empress. But who do *I* want to be? My master freed me. Last night I walked among the dead and my true friend spoke to me. Can *you* speak to me, God of Truth? If you'll only speak to me, I offer you—"

And then, it came to me.

The God had already spoken to me, before I had even asked.

The Lady Poppaea Sabina had used me to become Empress, but she had overplayed her hand.

Wasn't that what the Lady Statilia Messalina was hinting at? If I could only deflect the Divinitas's attentions onto someone else ... would I not be able to wriggle free of the retiarius's net?

"Go give the birds back," I said to Simon. "I already have my answer."

"Give them back?" I could hear the vendor's boy whining. "We don't give refunds."

"Yes, you do," Simon said. "Look, there's a blemish. A thousand sesterces! Shame on you, selling sullied shit in a sacred place."

He argued so belligerently on my behalf I resolved to hold off on the ten lashes until the boy did something *really* bad. I wondered whether that would make me a bad dominus. Compassion, after all, was not really a Roman virtue.

XXIII

STATILIA MESSALINA

The best way to find out more about Statilia Messalina would be the baths, meaning I would have to go in the morning, during the women's hours. The earlier the better, perhaps.

First, I found out from Nero's spies, who watched Petronius's house at all times, what the Divinitas planned for the next few days, for he was still entertaining the King of Armenia, and there were banquets, some public, some intimate, a poetry reading, as well as visits to the chariot races, the theater, and more games.

Croesus suggested the Baths of Agrippa rather than the newer Thermae Neronis; the family of Atticus were creatures of habit.

I left my boys in the palaestra, where they could find other youths to play and exercise with. They stripped down and joined some other youths. They were running and laughing and playing as though they were free. I was glad I had not let Simon get whipped; the stripes would have given him away.

I took Spider into the thermae. Taking Croesus's advice, I played the role of Empress to the hilt.

I had come to the baths wearing a silken stola, and veiled, as though announcing to the world that I was so important I had to come incognito. If anyone thought ill of my attire, they did not dare to say anything to someone so impressively dressed.

I took the women's entrance and was admitted without question, then into the apodyteria, with Spider fussing over me. Once in the changing area, I avoided disrobing completely. I shed my stola and the tunica beneath, and quickly wrapped myself discreetly in my palla, hiding any suspicious body parts. If any of the slaves in the apodyteria had noticed, or wanted to gossip, let them.

Two slaves brought me a pile of linen towels and then I draped myself quite thoroughly, handing over the palla for safekeeping.

I tipped them a quadrans each and told them to watch my clothes.

The robes the slaves were guarding, piled up in different corners of the antechamber, were a king's ransom in themselves; if it were not for the deterrent of summary crucifixion, there were probably plenty of would-be thieves in the thermae.

Spider asked one of them if the Lady Statilia Messalina had been seen that morning. We were told that she was there somewhere. The apodyteria had doors leading to chambers of varying temperatures. I did not want to seem to be looking for anyone in particular.

First we entered the caldarium and the heat hit so hard I immediately wanted to shed my towels, though I knew better. There were women of all sizes and complexions; naked, or nearly so, all sweating mightily or soaking in the hot water, they did not seem to be plebeians or patricians. The bath was truly the leveller, the thing all Roman citizens had in common. I had not really known this, because when I came to Rome I was a slave, and after that, I had only been in the house of Petronius, who was rich enough to bathe alone, and rarely sought the company of any but his own guests.

It was better for Spider to ask the questions, flitting between the groups of women and speaking only to the slaves. She ascertained that the Lady Statilia Messalina had been through the caldarium already.

In the frigidarium, it was too cold for gossiping. The floor mosaics depicted wild sea-creatures: giant octopuses, dolphins, Neptune waving his trident. The women were in huddles, in different corners. Some were braving the cold water of the pool. The sound of women chattering seemed to come from the next room; no doubt because it was the one with the most amenable temperature for chitchat.

We made our way to the tepidarium. Here, the walls showed scenes of domestic bliss, real or fanciful — Jupiter and Juno, Ulysses and Penelope, Augustus and Livia.

More women here, sitting in groups of two or three. A few had their own slaves tending to them. Others were making use of the public slaves, some for a little more than merely a massage. It was a secret world, like the sacred mysteries. And I stood at the boundary. If I chose, I could belong here too.

We spotted the lady. She lay on cushions laid out on the marble. A slave was rubbing scented olive oil onto her back; another was scraping the oil off with a strigil. A dumpling-shaped friend squatted beside her. The friend looked up and saw me.

"Wait, Statilia," she said, "I think you've won the bet after all. I'll leave you, then."

"Not yet, Vipsanilla," Statilia murmured. But the friend left her, laughing, and joined another gaggle.

"Enough," she said to the slaves. She stood, nude, and smiled at me briefly. Then she looked away. Then she went to the edge of the pool of lukewarm water, and waited for me to approach her. She did not call my name, playing along with my charade.

No, she did not look like Poppaea, except for the eyes. But the eyes would be enough.

I had not been wrong when I saw her last night. She would be perfect for my plans. She had spirit; Nero liked spirit. She was bossy. Nero would not like a woman who did not in some way resemble his mother.

For this was, in essence, what I needed to do. If I could deflect the Divinitas's attention to another woman … not that *I* was a woman, but Himself had begun seeing me as Poppaea, he could avoid thinking he had killed his wife … perhaps I could get past the changing of my voice. By then, it would be too late to castrate me.

Statilia Messalina barely glanced at me. She had taken it for granted that I would come.

"The doves," she said, still looking away. "Did you get the answer you wanted?"

"I got my answer without having to sacrifice," I said.

"You gave them back!" She turned to look at me at last.

"They said no refunds."

"Just like a slave," she said. "Money, money, money."

"I'm free," I said.

"You are not," she said, speaking the truth that I knew deep inside. "Can you get me an invitation?"

"He needs a wife." I did not add, any wife but me.

She said, "I have a husband."

"Will he mind?"

"My husband? He's not exactly in the Emperor's good graces right now; we haven't been seen at court for a year. And yet … I have known Lucius … intimately."

That did not surprise me. I did not think there was any woman of noble birth whom the Emperor had not at least sampled. With women he was omnivorous. With boys, I had learned, more selective. *Too* selective. Hence my predicament.

"Before you married your husband?" I asked her.

"Yes. Oh, a long time ago. But an old flame, I hope, can yet be fanned to life."

"Aren't you afraid?"

"I am not," said the Lady Statilia.

"Those whom the Divinitas loves…"

"Yes, I know. But you're still here."

"I wouldn't call it love. He *loved* the Lady Poppaea Sabina. Me, I don't think so. It is something akin to *need*."

"Well, it is true that he *needs* an Empress. And really, you won't do. He is not so insane as to think that your lowly birth and slavish origins qualify you to be anything but a toy. Not to mention that you have a penis."

"Exactly," I said.

Suddenly her eyes widened and she looked at me in a new way. She pulled me down to sit beside her. "You've *had* him, haven't you?"

I could not imagine how she knew.

"Just once."

"Why, that effeminate, ignoble, pathetic little cinaedus!" She laughed. "No offense."

"None taken, Lady Statilia." I understood her distaste. It's my place to be penetrated. But the Divinitas — proper Romans of standing don't debase their manhood that way. They become objects of derision. And for an *Emperor* ....

"Yet I have heard, from my slaves, that that is by no means an inviolate rule in other, less exalted cultures. The Celts, for instance, like to take turns. The Nubians, I have heard, do not discriminate one hole from another. As for the Greeks, they are *eromenoi* as youths, then once they grow beards, become the aggressors."

I knew little of those other worlds, having had my childhood, indeed my very selfhood, stolen from me on that pirate ship.

"You know a great deal," I said.

"I have little to do," she said, "except read."

"He likes women who appreciate good poetry," I said.

I had studied the Lady Poppaea Sabina quite thoroughly in her machinations to become Empress. Now, to avoid Poppaea's fate, I would need to use everything I had learned.

One advantage was that the Lady Statilia Messalina was in no way my friend. She was a means to an end. No doubt, Poppaea had seen me that way as well, in the beginning, but she and I had always had a kind of bond. I would not be in this predicament, perhaps, if I had not felt a kind of love for her. I could not allow myself any sympathy for this woman, or any kind of affection. But she was haughty. She was not easy to like.

To the Emperor, I was just an extension of Poppaea. Surely, I thought, a new distraction would allow me to escape. I did not belong in these political wars, these cosmic battles for power. I was happier to be nobody.

"He's having a private reading tonight," I said. "I'll ask Epaphroditus to put you on the list."

"You'll have to invite Atticus," said Statilia. "And Atticus has no ear for poetry at all. Surely there's a chariot race coming up?"

XXIV

POPPAEA OF THE STARLIGHT

When next I saw the Emperor, his mood had changed again. He was now in deep mourning. He wore an unwashed toga pulla, had not shaved, nor had an ornatrix been summoned to beautify his hair.

We were in a private dining room in the palace (so far, I had not dined in the same room twice there) and there were only eighteen at table; Tiridates was among them, and, as Epaphroditus had promised me, Atticus and Statilia had been invited to the gathering, but had been relegated to the second table.

Having not been told in advance about the mournful nature of the evening, the couple I had invited stood out. Atticus wore purple threaded with gold, which was his right as a once victorious general, and Statilia had her hair piled up almost as high as an obelisk, and sported an emerald fibula.

I myself had been told just in time, so I managed to find a drab grey tunica in time. When I arrived, I was immediately sent by Epaphroditus to the head couch, and made to sit between Tiridates and Himself, who only gave me a cursory acknowledgment.

I snuggled up to Himself — he seemed to want that — and let him sob into a fold of my tunica. "I've written a poem for tonight," he whispered.

"I can't wait to hear you read it, Lucius," I whispered back. But there was no kithara on the couch, and no back-up players to add resonance to his performance.

Overhearing, Tiridates said, "It's a very special poem indeed … so special, he won't even read it himself." And that was … unlike Himself, to say the least. What poem was so special that this author dared not read it?

I was to find out. Between the two sets of three couches, in the space between the two tables, stepped the Goddess Venus herself. She was taller than an ordinary woman, and painted completely in white lead paint, as though she were made of marble. She wore robes entirely dipped in purple. A palla was of purple, too, but stitched with stars in gold thread.

When she spoke, the voice was eerie, high, mellifluous, as though the stars themselves could speak. But the rhythm of the hexameters, the precise modulation of the Greek, the way each word was colored so as to seem to bring its innermost meaning to vivid life … that was Lucius Domitius Paris, the one performer that everyone secretly whispered was better than the Divinitas.

The one artist Nero knew in his heart was greater than he was.

In the poem, Venus, called Aphrodite as the ode was composed in Greek, descends in a chariot drawn by fantastical creatures: gryphons, lynxes, sphinxes, dragons, each animal brought to life with a few well-chosen adjectives and a vocal embellishment.

Lucius *was* the Goddess. He wasn't just impersonating a woman. He was all that a woman is. The transformation was astounding, even more so than what we had seen in the Theater of Pompey. I knew I could never do that.

In the poem, Aphrodite descends into the cubiculum of Poppaea Sabina, heavy with child. I think the Chrestianoi have a similar story about one of their heavenly messengers visiting their version of Magna Mater. The Goddess invites Poppaea to ascend with her in the chariot:

Make haste and weep no more
The myriad stars of Zeus's heaven
are bidding you welcome …
they will enthrone you
on the moon's fair face …

But Poppaea is unwilling. Her love for Nero is too great. But the Goddess tells her

Do not be downcast
at the favor shown you
Though your husband is a man
equal to the gods

and

On this earth your two children

have passed away
Among the gods
you shall watch them
for all eternity

Then the song continued with Poppaea's apotheosis. She rode to the stars in the celestial chariot. She was greeted by a shower of shooting stars and a symphonia of starlight, represented by a chorus of concealed young boys, their voices soaring over the twanging of kitharas and the whine of double flutes.

We were in tears. It was if I was witnessing firsthand the transformation of woman into Goddess. As I listened, I remembered our first meeting. I remembered how we had pleasured each other while her first husband lay, fat and snoring, in the same bed. I remembered that in her strange way, she had been a friend to me, and she had wanted to talk to me in the end, not him, not the agent of her violent death.

I was wrapped in the arms of that agent. Hot tears spurted from his eyes and moistened my face. I was crying, too.

"You knew her, Sporus," the God whispered to me. "And soon you will know her even better."

I summoned a nearby delicatus and told him to pour a krater of snow-chilled, strong Falernian. I held it to the Emperor's lips. He sipped at it, and his tears mingled with the wine.

"Is he not a great artist?" said Nero.

I knew that my duty was now to say, "But not so great as you, Divinitas," but I could not force it from my lips. So I said nothing and smiled.

I knew that the scraped-off sweat of gladiators and charioteers commanded a hefty premium in the apothecaries' market.

I noted that he was not uninterested in Statilia Messalina. I just needed to push a little harder.

After the poetry evening, I was not summoned to the Imperial cubiculum. I was relieved. I called for my litter, thinking I could sleep in Petronius's house. But as I was leaving, I was intercepted by Marcus.

"Himself has asked for you," he told me.

"Another trip through the suburra?" I asked, thinking that Himself wanted to work through his grief with another night of debauchery.

But then I saw that a large entourage was assembling: senators, Epaphroditus and his stoic protégé Epictetus, and an Egyptian priest.

"No," said the master of the world, emerging from an inner room. "No ribaldry tonight. We are going to pay a visit to the Lady Poppaea Sabina."

XXV

POPPAEA OF THE DAWN

Thus it was that I learned that the Lady Poppaea Sabina would not be cremated like any other Roman. The guests followed the Emperor, some on foot, some in litters. I sat with the Divinitas. I could not fathom his emotion.

Our litters bore us down an underground passageway that branched, here and there. There were sporadic brackets with torches, some already spent. I would not have known where we were going but for overhearing the litter-bearers and their foreman telling them where to turn. There was a network of such passageways. That was why the Divinitas, or the Praetorians, could seem to appear anywhere in the city, by magic.

Where we emerged was Regio III, Isis and Serapis, not far from where Nero's Golden House was taking shape. But we were still underground. We had reached a huge subterranean chamber, the walls painted in Egyptian style.

We stepped from our litter. It was just myself and the Divinitas.

'Where's my audience?" said Nero.

They were far behind us, hanging back. Something awkward was about to happen and no one dared presume to follow the Emperor.

Epictetus limped forward and pushed a door open. Only Nero and I stepped through. I was conscious that others, lining the corridor outside, were observing. Whispering.

A monumental statue of Anubis dominated the chamber. The walls were covered in hieroglyphics. A bald priest was working on a body that was mostly covered with a linen sheet. I could not identify who it was. To my horror, he was extracting the corpse's brains through its nose, and placing them in an alabaster jar.

In another corner, a painter was at work, creating a portrait on a panel made of cartonnage, the papyrus-and-plaster material for funerary masks. The image of the woman's face was emerging from swirls of paint, so lifelike I almost believed the lips were moving.

I knew who it must be lying there.

The priest moved and an arm slid past the linen covering. I could see a hand against the side of the table. I knew the hand. The hand had caressed the most intimate parts of me.

It was a delicate hand. It was in fact, my own hand, almost.

"Poppaea," the Emperor whispered.

He took my hand and led me to the table. The priest wiped some viscous fluid from the nostril and drew back the drape. Poppaea Sabina lay there with her eyes closed.

Nero pulled the drape away completely. There was an incision through which they had removed her internal organs, but it was sewn shut and barely visible because white leaden paint coated her whole body. There was a powerful perfume masking the whiff of decay, blending with the clouds of frankincense from braziers set at the room's four corners. In the flickering light, in the fog of incense, she was a marble goddess.

The Divinitas pushed me against the side of the table and, caressing me with one hand, half climbed up over the Empress's corpse. I was terrified. Dead, Poppaea's flesh seemed to suck my life force, seemed to animate itself through the racing of my blood, my labored breath.

How could this be happening, with half the court behind the half-open door, voyeurs, tittering? I was humiliated beyond imagining, but then again, I was nothing. I believed I would be killed. His face was contorted, almost unrecognizable.

The Emperor cried out, screams of rage, pain, grief, desire and guilt, all these feelings, gushing out all at once. I could feel all these things. In my terror, I was as frozen as the dead Empress. I felt not only fear but pity. The master of the world was desperate to be loved and all he had was a dead wife and an ex-slave. I knelt against the cold stone of the slab, the one conscious receptacle of the God's despair.

Then Nero Claudius Caesar Augustus Germanicus shuddered and became still for a moment. Then he stood up and turned away from me. He did not even look at me. I swabbed my stained face and hair with the sleeve of my tunica. At this moment I was of no more import than a vase or a bowl, or a rag used to wipe away the traces of someone's lovemaking.

I was nothing. But I too have needs.

Deep inside, past all the layers that others have constructed, past the mirrors piled atop mirrors in which my owners have seen their own selves reflected, I too am a person.

And in that moment, that person was seen by no one. No one in this world.

Why then should *I* acknowledge that person? I thought. Better to play my appointed role.

"Lucius," I whispered.

Slowly he turned. I stood beside the dead Imperatrix, my tunica ripped. He did not even see me. He heard me as though it were *her* voice. And he said, "I'll make you a goddess."

"Yes," I said. "Put me up there, among the stars."

"I will," he said.

And so you became Empress.

I did not. Not at all. Not even close. On the contrary. I was, for a time, forgotten. I took little part in the elaborate rituals of the Lady Poppaea's Egyptian-style funeral.

I was not of course allowed in the Senate, so I was not there when they proclaimed her a goddess, but I was in the background with the bulk of the entourage when a portion of the temple of Serapis was rededicated for her cult and her new-minted priests performed their first sacrifices, a white heifer and also a white calf, to honor her stillborn child who was deified as a kind of afterthought.

The Romans can make gods just by passing a law.

They can unmake them, too.

You mean the Damnatio Memoriae decreed for my erstwhile husband.

A decree is making you *a god.*

A god for an hour, followed by violent death.

I don't believe in gods like these. They drink the blood of sacrificial animals and offer vague promises in return. I think that a man can be a god, but I don't think you can be a god if some old men decree it.

Was Nero a God?

There were times when I felt it.

And I felt it that day, violated, tossed aside, by a power as elemental as thunder or a tempest.

I saw the emptiness inside the God, and I knew that the abyss could never be filled. It would devour me utterly. And yet, as I have said, I too have needs.

Oh, I hated him. I hated what he had made me. I hated what I had become because of him. And yet, beneath that hate, there was still the spark I felt when I first heard him sing. There was a kind of love.

Such delicious ironies your life held! Oh, I am jealous. I am an artist, and yet my work is smudged or sweated into oblivion in a day. My beautiful transforming of you from prisoner to goddess won't even live a day before you're ripped to shreds by the rapist … oh! Did I offend? So many jobs for these arena reenactments … you get jaded.

You're not talking.

I don't blame you for getting sullen. Don't get all soggy though, or I will have to do your face again. Try not to think about it. All right. Don't say anything.

***

That day, the Emperor left in his litter, down the subterranean tunnel. I heard footsteps. People had been peeking. They might not have seen anything, but they had guessed that it was something dark, something unthinkable.

The door slammed shut. I was by myself.

Not exactly by myself; priests were still chanting, the painter was still working on the portrait, and the mummifier-in-chief had gone back to working on the dead body of the former Imperatrix.

I went upstairs, into the dawn. Stepping out of the old Temple of Isis and Serapis, I got my bearings, and I slowly made my way back to the house of my former master.

I was not summoned for some weeks; and then it was not by the Divinitas, but by the one who planned to become the new Empress of Rome, the Lady Statilia Messalina.

XXVI

The Judgment of Paris

I was dejected. I was depressed. I was disillusioned.

For days, I lay in my former master's cubiculum.

Croesus brought me wine, which I did not touch, and later, poppy juice from Ephesus, which I did. They say it will send you to a world from which you will never wish to return.

I drifted, drifted, drifted on a cloud of semiconsciousness. I drifted and willed myself not to awaken.

I dreamed. I saw Hyacinth again. This time, he did not speak to me, but I saw him, running across green fields. I saw him but he did not see me. He ran free and did not seem to know me anymore. He was naked. He was whole.

In the afterlife, or at least in my dream, his identity had not been sliced from him.

I think I saw my mother, but I was no longer sure if I even recognized her. It could have been Spider. It could even have been Poppaea.

I saw pirates being crucified beside the churning sea.

Each dream was a mosaic stone in the convoluted picture of my life.

And then there was another dream … a dream that retold the story of my life in Rome.

First, more floating. Clouds. Celestial music. The lyre, the kithara, the double flute, the tympanon.

And as I floated, I reached the slopes of a mountain. The sky was impossibly blue, almost painfully bright. A warm wind buoyed me as I sailed the sunlight.

I was in a grove. There were Corinthian columns. Three goddess stood, naked, and a chubby man in a purple toga was polishing an apple with a fold of his cloak.

Each goddess was perfect. Each stood in the tall grass under the laurel trees, each smiled, each had sunlight in her eyes and the warm breeze in her hair, each spoke with a voice that was music.

The first goddess was the Lady Octavia, primly dressed, perfectly coifed. "Choose me," she said. "I'll give you access to the reins of power. I am the true descendant of the Julio-Claudians, not an adopted misfit like you. Choose me," she said. "You will be victorious in war." The Lady Octavia was playing the role of Minerva, goddess of war and wisdom. Nero's legitimacy hung on Octavia's bloodline.

I was visiting a distorted reenactment of the Judgment of Paris. Paris had to choose to give the golden apple to whichever goddess was the most beautiful — and each goddess came with a gift. In the story, it is the gift that decides, not the beauty ....

In this grove of dreams, mythology was playing itself out as though on a stage. Indeed, there was something of Lucius Domitius Paris in all of the goddess-women; they were being, as it were, *impersonated.*

Next, you see, there was the Lady Statilia Messalina, who said, "I will be whatever you tell me to be; I will give you submission, I will give you steadfast support, wise and truthful advice, I will gladly suffer your infidelities, only call me Imperatrix."

She was playing the role of Hera, who put up with Jupiter's amours with princesses, nymphs, and boys, yet never relinquished the title of Queen of the Gods.

And the third was the one who was almost my friend, Poppaea Sabina, who stood in the center, massively pregnant yet still irresistible.

The Lady Poppaea Sabina was Venus, who promised Paris the most beautiful woman in the world.

"You *know,"* she said, "what I can give you. That's why you're going to choose me, no matter what."

Paris, the shepherd boy, who was Nero, the God, was played in my dream by Lucius Domitius Paris, an actor whose name was both that of the myth and that of the Emperor. He was playing *all* the roles in this dream-play. And all of them to perfection. The three goddesses and the god-emperor ... all one actor, all perfectly distinguished yet somehow the same. I watched the scene, peering from a branch of a laurel tree.

It's a dream and it's past and present and future all blended together.

Nero-Paris says to Octavia, "You can't give me anything. You haven't got a head." And a bolt of lightning from a clear sky strikes off the Empress's head. The head rolled to a stop at the foot of the tree.

There I am, holding my breath, hoping I won't be seen. I may be dreaming, but I don't want any part of this infernal game. I know my Homer by now. This game sparks the Trojan War and endless death, and the destruction of entire civilizations.

To Statilia, Nero-Paris says, "Yes, you're steady and calming. But boring. So boring I bet you'll even survive me."

"Which leaves me," says the Lady Poppaea, whom I last remember reclining on a slab of marble. Supremely confident, she moves toward him. Her belly swells. She staggers. She tries to embrace him but he hurls another lightning-bolt.

"Agrippina!" she screams.

Poppaea splits in two and from the two bloody halves steps another Poppaea and I see now that *I* am that Poppaea. I'm no longer a watcher in this dream but the subject of the dream. Jupiter the Thunderer sends rainfall and washes the slick blood from my perfect, pristine body.

And as I walk towards him, my arms outstretched, both longing for and dreading the embrace of Divinity … the sun is impossibly bright … the wind is warm against my body … I whisper *Lucius, Lucius* and he responds … his lips open to kiss … it's beautiful for only a few moments, then his jaws expand until they they seem to swallow me, they are a ravening maw, devouring me, sucking me down into the burning heart of a volcano.

Poppaea.

I scream and —

That's when the dream faded, and I found myself sleeping on my former dominus's bed, the sheet drenched in sweat, blood, tears, and vomit.

"More of that posset," I murmured, believing that the poppy juice would send me deep into oblivion.

"Enough," Croesus said.

Simon and Hylas were wiping my brow, and Croesus was cleaning me with a sponge dipped in watered-down sour wine. And Spider was there too, telling me it was time to get up, get out and about.

"You haven't risen for three days," Croesus said.

"The palace?" I said.

"No summons. The Divinitas has been spending all his time with Statilia Messalina."

Had my ruse worked? Had the Divine Eye finally wandered away from me? I did not dare hope. But today, at least, I was still free.

"Will you take the air, domine?" Hylas asked me.

"Yes," I said. "Give me a bath. And tell the litter-bearers to stand by."

I noted that Hylas was now addressing me in grammatically correct Latin.

And Hylas saw that I was finally giving him orders, like a proper dominus. He grinned. But I felt a twinge of discomfort, though I knew it was the way of things.

XXVII

THE TEMPLE OF CASTOR AND POLLUX

It had been the nones of the month when I left the Temple of Isis and Serapis. By the time I left the house of Petronius, it was close to the ides.

Too weak to walk far as yet, I was glad of the litter. I set off without any particular goal, but inevitably, most streets in Rome end up in the Forum. There were the crowds, the colors and especially the smells: the sour wine, the foul wind from the cloaca, the smoke of grilled sausages, the whiff of a whore's perfume, the fragrance of fresh-baked bread.

I told the bearers to wait in an alley near the back of the Temple of Castor and Pollux, the Dioscuri. Telling Hylas to wait with the litter, I took Simon with me in case I bought something and needed someone to carry it. I thought I might shop my way across the grassy square and down the Via Sacra. Such a mundane pleasure, and yet I had never experienced it as a freedman. Just being able to

"I am an Emperor. I must have an Empress. Zeus has Hera. Cronos had Rhea. Uranus had Gaia. There can be no sky that is not grounded by the earth. I am the sheltering sky of Rome, and I must have a bride. Or … when it rains, who will receive the seed?"

I waited, apprehension gnawing at the pit of my stomach.

At length, I said, "What do you think of Statilia Messalina?"

"Oh!" he pursed his lips. "I fucked her once."

"I took the liberty of inviting her."

I indicated the opposite couch. The Lady Statilia had been placed in the direct eyeline of the Emperor, who had not noticed only because Paris's monodrama was playing out between the two tables. But now, the song was ending, and Paris was prostrating himself in the most toadying *proskinesis*, while the choir boys and musicians also came in from left and right and prostrated themselves.

He could see her clearly for the first time. A woman like Statilia Messalina always knows when she's being looked at. She smiled at him.

"Her husband," the Emperor said to me, "is an illiterate bore. Could you not have brought her alone?"

"He's old-fashioned," I said. "An old-style *paterfamilias* type."

"Have them come to the races," he said.

"But you're competing yourself," I said, thinking that it would hardly be a good moment to plan an assignation.

"Even better. The sweat of the arena is the best aphrodisiac."

squeeze two fruits to see which was the riper! Or to pick up a kylix and ask the price, or taste a sausage without being ordered to!

Then I thought of myself in Simon's place, and I said, "If you want something for yourself, go ahead, buy it." So we stopped at a toy stand and he chose a little wooden chariot. It was an ingenious thing, cunningly carved from a single piece of wood, and cost a whole denarius. He grinned from ear to ear, clutching it in his fist. I understood how he felt. I had never had a toy like that either.

Then I heard a crier in the distance: "Boy for sale!" above the hubbub. "Let's get back," I said to my own boy, but Simon seemed rooted to the spot.

"Come, Simon, this isn't a slave market, it's just some random man selling off his—" Then I remembered that Simon's own father had sold him off to pay a gambling debt. "Simon," I said, "did you say that your father tried to sell you twice? And that your brother was sold … and died?"

"Yes, domine."

"You have more brothers?"

"I — I don't know. My father has many women."

I put my arm on his shoulder and tried to steer him away. But at that moment, a boy was pushing his way through the mob, and in pursuit, there was a bearded man wearing a robe that did not seem cheap — not the kind of man who needed to pawn his children for cash.

The boy was running straight for us, and there was nothing behind us but the toy stall and the Temple of the Dioscuri. He crashed into a pile of dolls and, unable to go further, turned to face his pursuer.

"You already sold me twice," he said. "It's illegal for you to sell your children three times."

People around us started talking. "He's right, you know." "What sort of a father —" "Shame on you!" "He's within his rights, he's the paterfamilias," and that sort of thing.

The boy dived under the stand and crouched there, shaking.

The man noticed, then, the boy standing next to me. He transformed from a creature of rage to a kind of exaggerated joy, beaming with pleasure. "And I thought you lost, Simon," he said.

"Leave me alone, abba," Simon said.

"It is true that your little brother has been sold three times. Of course, he is a lot better-looking than you are, so I was able to realize a higher payment for a shorter period of servitude. So, let him go. I'll sell you." Loudly he cried out, "I have another one for sale here. He can read and write, oh, yes, many languages. And he has only been sold once. Well, technically, twice."

"Stop!" I said. "Technically, three times. I paid both those repulsive men off."

"You?" he sneered. "You never paid *me*. Third-party sales are not covered by the law of patria potestas."

That could well have been true, for all I knew. What did I know of the finer points of their legal system? Yet, how many laws did the Divinitas break every morning before breakfast?

Simon said, "I have a good dominus. He never even beats me!"

Simon's father began laughing.

"He bought me this," Simon said, opening his fist to reveal the little chariot.

"Toys!" said his father. He raised his fist, but hesitated when I looked at him threateningly. Like all bullies, he was at heart a fearful man. "And what do you do for your dominus that gets you toys? What do you do for him, you filthy little cinaedus? Your master seems little more than a painted whore himself. What can he see in you?"

"If you must know," I said, "he tutors my household staff in Latin and Greek."

"By the Gods!" the man said, his laughter turning into lusty guffaws.

"Don't swear, abba," said the boy. Then added something in their own language which was, I think, Aramaic. His father grew incensed.

"In that case," he said, "a thousand sesterces and you can have them both."

"I'll have my steward draw up the note," I said.

At that moment, a man stepped out through the crowd. I could have sworn I knew him. But he wore a toga, and I realized when I last saw him he was of much lower estate, certainly not a citizen. And he spoke to me in the tongue of my people.

"Don't give him a brass as," he said, and then he called me by my real name.

"Viridian!" I cried, astonished, for I recognized him as once being the slave of the old poet Seneca, Nero's tutor, who had long since been disposed of in Tigellinus's purge of Pisonian conspirators.

He spoke, his voice imbued with a gravitas that stilled dissent. "I am," he said, "Lucius Annaeus Seneca Lucii

Libertus Viridianus, an advocatus and one of the jure consulti of the Imperial household."

Turning to Simon's father, he said, "You, sir, are —?

"Josephus," the man said, stammering a little. "I'm a poor baker, and this man — boy, really — is trying to stop me from exercising my legal rights."

"The younger one is lost to you completely. The law is unambiguous. Your parental rights were dissolved as soon as the third sale occurred. As for this one, however —"

"Wait!" I whispered. "Aren't you trying to help me?"

He appeared to ignore me and continued suavely, "You perhaps have a point, Josephus, when you point out that the third sale of this son was not consummated directly with you. It could theoretically be argued, then, that you have a right to sell him to this man, or any other, if you so choose."

"All right, then," Josephus said. "A thousand."

Simon clutched my arm tightly. He started to cry.

"Well yes, but this man, Sporus, also has a case. It would have to be argued before a magistrate. As one of the city's most accomplished lawyers, I would almost certainly win the case, but the law is never entirely certain. And my fees — ah, my fees —"

"Charge what you want!" Josephus said. "Just leave me enough to pay off my losing at dice last night."

"Well, my normal fee for a difficult case like this would be about two thousand sesterces, plus expenses, of course."

"That's all right then. I don't need a lawyer."

"But the young man, who is the Emperor's favorite and has access to the privy purse, would certainly want to take *you* to court, as he claims to own this boy already," Viridian said. "And I'm pretty sure he can afford my fee."

"By the pudenda of Venus, I can afford it!" I said. "Double it. Double whatever that bastard says he can pay."

"I only take coin," Viridian added. "Were you planning to pay me in loaves?"

"Have mercy," said Josephus. "Do you know how much it costs to feed and clothe a child? And the boy's been sneaking off to be with the lowest elements — pickpockets, whores, and Chrestianoi even! That's his latest hobby! He'll be thrown to the lions in no time, and where's my investment, all that food, the clothing, the love, the care, the tenderness!"

"Love! Tenderness! A turd for your tenderness! My dominus loves me more than you'll ever understand," Simon screamed.

"Of course he does. You're an investment."

"Your only investment is in the dice."

"All right! Forget all this!" Josephus said. "I'll go. I need to pay my debts, but I have a daughter."

"But attempting to sell your child a third time is also punishable," Viridian said. "What is to prevent me from having you arrested? Plenty of these good people watching this altercation would be happy to go and fetch one of the vigiles."

At this, Josephus stalked off in a rage, and the crowd started applauding.

"Good riddance!" Simon shouted. To me he said, "You see — I have a *khara* for a father."

As that died down, I could not help overhearing other kinds of whispers ... like, "Isn't that Nero's boy?" "Doesn't he look just like her, though!" "He's a good boy." "He'll keep the Divinitas from flying off the handle." "He's pretty!" "Does he charge the Emperor by the hour?" and such, flattering and derogatory, all of it making me squeamishly aware that every moment I was in public, I was being observed.

"Lucius Viridianus," I said softly, "thank you for coming to the child's rescue."

"My rescue, too, domine," said Simon.

"But where did he go?" I said.

For though he had been cowering beneath the toy-stall, that child was gone. I needed to find him, perhaps to bring him under my protection. He and Simon should be together, I thought. I should free them all, I thought. I had been like them. I knew what they knew. I knew what it was to be a thing.

"Don't worry about the boy," Viridian said.

"You knew about him!" Simon exclaimed. "You know where he's headed … you were coming to rescue him, weren't you? Please, domine, what's he to you? Is he your lover?"

"Hardly!" Viridian laughed a little. "He's my brother," he said.

And then I understood completely. "You're a Chrestianos. You, him, you're all part of that cannibal cult from Judaea."

"Not me," Simon said quickly.

"Are you going to turn me in, Sporus?" said Viridian.

I did not answer. He knew I would not. How did he know? He and I were brothers too, in a way, as much as being fellow members of a mystery cult.

"Well," he said, "that's settled. Perhaps, Simon, you would like to meet your brother properly?"

XXVIII

CHRESTIANOI

Viridian had a litter nearby, not quite as ostentatious as mine of course, but we followed him quickly through the maze until we reached a five-story insula at the foot of the Capitoline, a prime location for such humble dwellings.

We hopped out, and Viridian opened the front door himself. When I looked curiously at him, he said, "I don't have any slaves."

"At all?"

There were a few people about who appeared to be in some kind of servile status. But that was not the surprise. The surprise was that this was no insula. The ground floor of an insula usually has several apartments; it's the most livable of the floors because the city's water and sanitation systems often do not reach the upper levels. But this insula was hollowed out and while it was brick and timber on the outside, and shabby to say the least, and the foyer with its stairs leading up to the higher stories was nondescript ...

once a double doorway was opened we stepped into an interior that was decorated like an aristocrat's dwelling.

"But, Viridian," I asked, "with all the rewards from your advocacy, why do you not move to a proper domus?"

"As you well know, Sporus," Viridian said, "respectable people don't *work* for a living. Imagine all my neighbors if I were to move to a domus! They would turn up their noses!"

There were no lares and penates, but there was bust of Seneca where the ancestors would normally be, and a colonnaded inner garden with rose bushes and an imported citrus tree.

"From Judaea," Simon said, in awe. He ran toward the tree.

"Would you like to send your people home?" Viridian said to me in my own language. "I can send you home in my own litter afterwards. Slaves feel strange in a house with no slaves. I would hate for them to become infected with revolutionary ideas. I know they love you, but love is never as powerful as freedom."

I told my litterbearers, and Hylas, to go back. Simon of course would have to remain; this visit was all about his half-brother, after all. But first, my slaves were treated to an amphora of wine and a basket of bread and fish.

"I'll have the men carry this stuff," Hylas said. "We don't want to stink up the inside of your litter."

"You're generous," I said to Viridian.

Viridian replied, "Our teacher taught us that we should always do to others what we would have them do to ourselves."

"Oh!" said Simon, unable to help himself. "You're a Jew!" To me he said, "He's quoting Rabbi Hillel, one of our most beloved learned men."

"A Jew?" Viridian said. "Well, I suppose you might call it that. At least, I have learned from Jews. But you know very well that I am from the same land Sporus comes from."

In the center of the garden, stone steps led to an underground chamber, and a door in the chamber opened to another descending stairway. We saw a tunnel, crudely hollowed from rock, leading to darkness. On either side of the tunnel, a torch glowed in a bracket. Viridian gave one of them to Simon and told him to walk ahead.

The tunnel broadened. Now there were niches in the rock, and a faint odor of decay. "This is Jewish burial place," Simon whispered. "You *are* one of us."

"Your people are not the only ones who use these catacumbae," Viridian said. "They've proved useful for the Chrestianoi, too."

"I've heard," I said, "that there are secret places where they ... *you* ... practice your rituals."

"Oh, the cannibal love-feasts, shitting on the portraits of Caesar, orgies, and all the other rumors," Viridian said. "I've heard those rumors too."

We turned a corner. There were more niches now, and the smell of death was more pervasive, and it was mixed with perfume and frankincense. In some of the niches lay the dead, tightly shrouded, some mummified and wearing masks that were painted with lifelike portraits, and there were also ossuaries, both of wood and of stone.

We heard a rustle. A sheet moved.

"You can come out," Viridian whispered.

Simon held up his torch. His half-brother, shivering, lay in a niche side by side with a loosely wrapped dead woman. He scrambled out.

"I didn't even know I had a brother," Simon said.

But the family resemblance was clear.

"My name is Adam," the boy said.

Placing his torch in the nearest bracket, Simon allowed his brother to embrace him. It was a diffident embrace, for they were two strangers who shared, unknowingly, a terrible father.

"Can he come and live with us?" Simon said.

"Why don't you ask *me?*" Adam said. "I'm not a slave."

"True," Viridian said, "he's been sold three times."

As he saw he was no longer in danger, Simon's brother became assertive. "I'll take the torch," he said. "It's not far."

We went down another passageway. The reek of the dead grew stronger and we were now in a wider chamber, with torches still lit. There were marble steles in Greek, Latin, and what must be some language of the east. Some niches had fresh flowers and small gifts: food, a toy, a scroll. The ceiling was high and the niches with bodies went all the way up. A ladder leaned against one wall; there was an opening, perhaps three stories of an insula overhead. Placing his torch in an empty bracket, Adam started to climb. We followed. It was precarious. I was nervous.

The opening led to a small room piled with jars of olive oil, a storeroom of some kind. Adam led us past the amphorae to a wooden door and we found ourselves in a kitchen. A group of men and women were sitting around a table and ... this was very odd ... they were of different walks of life. There was an aristocrat in a toga. Others looked like slaves, yet they sat at the same table in an unsettling sort of equality.

Adam said to Simon, "You see, these are my brothers as well."

Presently, there came a man who looked to be in his sixties, tall, bearded; he looked a little travel-weary. The women in the room made much of him and brought him wine and olives.

Adam whispered, "That man is called Cephas. He's come a long way to celebrate with us." And a celebration it was. They broke bread and shared it with me and Simon, and they sang songs; to my surprise, Simon knew some of them.

"So, Sporus, this is one of the cannibalistic orgies you've heard so much about," Viridian said to me, laughing.

Presently the man named Cephas began telling stories which he had heard from his own teacher, a man, who, he claimed, had come back from the dead; I had heard such tales before from other cults, for there were cults all over Rome; this one sounded a little bit like sun worshipping beliefs about Mithras, a little bit like the fertility rites of Adonis. Mixed in with these myths were homespun morality tales; when Petronius told me stories like these, they had the fire of poetry; these tales were more the kind of thing I might have heard in my old life, told by my mother.

It was my mother I thought of. She became suddenly very vivid to me. I had not thought of her, really, since the savage pirate broke me in to this new life. A tear came to my eye.

Viridian said, "Yes, it is moving, isn't it?"

I watched their faces, all rapt, all drawn into the old man's narrative. Hypnotized. I was unnerved. This was not my world. Then Cephas started to talk of a second coming, of the rule of Rome being replaced by the rule of their own God-King, and I could see how some might find subversion in all of it. I did not think they should all be thrown to lions, of course; but when they started to talk with glazed eyes about dead people coming back to rule the earth, it made me uncomfortable. Did they actually believe these things, or were these fantasies just their way of coping with the soullessness of a Rome now in its eighth century, a Rome that had swallowed up the whole world?

Yet I saw that Simon's brother was utterly absorbed in all this talk. Perhaps it was because he'd never known a real family, and these misfits were all he had.

If this was one of the infamous orgies these people indulged in, I would have to say that a slow day at the palace was wilder than this. I had to envy their sense of belonging, of solidarity, though, even as I felt they were being lulled into accepting their lot in exchange for a dubious promise of paradise.

But the love-feast was interrupted abruptly. We heard banging outside.

"Soldiers," Viridian whispered urgently to me. "Do you remember the way back?"

"Will you all go down and hide in the catacumbae?" I said.

"No, we'll face them. Now go."

"Adam, come," I said, grabbing the hand of my slave's brother.

"I'm staying," he said. "What am I to you? These people are my brothers and sisters."

Simon said, "And *I'm* your brother."

"Yes. Who you didn't even know about until today. Forget me," Adam said.

Adam pushed us toward the storeroom. He slammed the door. Holding back tears, Simon waited by the ladder for me, then we scrambled into the burial chamber. None of the Chrestianoi followed.

"They're mad, mad, *mad!*" Simon said, taking the torch from the bracket where he had left it. "Come, domine, I know the way." And he did. He had remembered every turn and he led me down the passageways without even pausing to think. It seemed to take no time at all to arrive at the garden in the insula that had been so bizarrely converted into a rich man's home.

The servants of Viridian, seeing we had returned without him, immediately knew that something had happened. Still, they arranged for me to take Viridian's own litter all the way to Petronius's house.

When we arrived, it was already the ninth hour. Pretorians were waiting outside my door. They had come to deliver an invitation to dinner.

But it was not an invitation to the palace. It was a request to dine at the home of the consul, Marcus Julius Vestinus Atticus. The invitation was not from this man, whose name I could barely place, but from his wife, the Lady Statilia Messalina.

My respite had been all too brief. It seemed that I was to plunge once more into the politics of power.

XXIX

MARCUS JULIUS VESTINUS ATTICUS

"May I decline the invitation?" I asked the guard.

"No," said the Praetorian, "we're to take you, regardless of the hour."

"But I don't even know this Atticus."

"The invitation is in his name. He's an old-fashioned person in a way. Doesn't think his wife should issue any pronouncements."

"That's about to change," said the Praetorian who was with him. No, the man with him was no mere guardsman. His tunic bore the broad laticlavus stripe of a tribune.

"In any case," said the first, "*Himself* wants you there."

"Boy or girl?" I asked.

"Didn't say."

"Simon, go in the house. Tell Hylas to prepare one of each," I said. To the tribune, I said, "Why has a tribune been sent to fetch a nobody like me?

"Oh, I'm not here for you," he said. "You were just on the way."

I did not want Hylas to go with me. If I took a slave who had the look of a puer delicatus, they would assume I had brought him to help out with the festivities, and I found increasingly disturbing the prospect of my slave, who was in some sense also my friend, being manhandled by some inebriated senator. Although to Hylas such things were just work. Slaves need feel no shame more keenly than the mere fact of their servitude.

"But domine," he was saying, "If you need to change your clothes —"

"If the likes of Nymphidius happened to be attending the Divinitas," I said, "you might be permanently damaged."

"Well, domine, if you're just protecting your property, then I understand. But I want to protect *you,* too."

"Your Greek is getting better every day. Stay home and work on your contracted verbs with Simon. I'd rather have you in pain over conjugating some verb in the second aorist than lanced by Nymphidius in a drunken fit."

I would have taken Spider, but perhaps there was perhaps a chance Himself would recognize that this was the woman who had been broken in the process of extracting information about the Vestal Virgin who had been his mistress.

In the end, it was Croesus I asked to accompany me. He was a freedman, a man who knew state secrets, and valuable enough, and wily enough, not to end up as a collateral victim should the Divinitas go on a rampage.

And he knew many of the Praetorians personally. He followed me on foot.

The domus of Atticus was positively spartan in comparison with other aristocrats'. Remembering that when I last saw him, the Emperor had been weeping over Poppaea, I had arrived wrapped from head to toe in a silk stola and with my hair coifed high, topped with a diamond diadem. My appearance was as far from the inspirational Giton of Petronius as could be imagined.

Leaving Croesus to gather what gossip he could among the house slaves, I allowed myself to be ushered into the banquet. Individual portions were being served up of a pie stuffed with flamingoes' tongues.

It was not that extravagant an affair. Just one set of couches, and all nine places were full, so I did not even have a seat. The other guests included the head Praetorians, Nymphidius and Tigellinus, and a few senators. An also, I noted, the Emperor's great-aunt, the terrifying hag who ruled over the Vestal Virgins. Though the Vestals had to preserve their chastity on pain of death, it appeared that indulgent banquets were not off limits.

I stood awkwardly at the entrance to the triclinium, whose frescoes depicted a staid, conventional mythological scene, I think of Diana, Jupiter, and the nymph Callisto in the process of being transformed into a bear. Behind me, there were the two Praetorians who had brought me. Rather unusually, they did not wait outside, but flanked me on either side, silently saluting their master.

A lone singer was accompanying herself on the lyre, singing the words of an ancient Greek poet:

I drink, Bacchos! I drink!

I drink deeper than the Cyclops Polyphemos
drinking the blood of men.

Could I but drink from your skull
and drain its blood,
O you who guzzles the blood
of your poisoned friends!

"A song about wine to be sure, but an ill-omened one," I said ... softly, I thought, and only to myself. But the music stopped abruptly. The God had raised his hand for silence.

"You don't like Alcaeus?" said Himself, sitting in between his hosts, the Lady Statilia Messalina whom I knew well and her husband, with whom I'd barely exchanged a word. If Statilia was overdressed, her husband was even more so, in military uniform no less, the brass polished until it was blinding, even in the candlelight.

Everyone waited.

"Who doesn't love Alcaeus?" I said, temporizing while I figured out which way the wind blew. There was tension in the room. "But ... I would hate to think of wine and poison in the same breath."

"Ah, my beautiful, witty, demoniacally clever wife," said the Ruler of the World. "Have you come from the dead, come to scold me? Is my mother with you?"

"I left her back in ... her tomb," I said softly.

The Emperor took from inside his toga a huge red jewel, carved into a circular spyglass, and peered at me for a while. Then he put away the ruby and tried a bright yellow topaz. He scrutinized me a little more, than bade me approach by crooking a finger. A crowd of slaves bearing platters of food parted to let me approach the table.

As I got closer, Himself put away his giant gemstones and began to laugh. After a second, everyone joined in, though none of them knew quite what was funny.

"Why, Poppaea, my beloved," said the Divinitas, "I wasn't expecting you. Rather, I was hoping to see that pretty boy who looks just like you. Can you conjure him up, perhaps?"

I played along. "It will almost be like magic," I said.

I stripped off the stola with a grandiose gesture and it fluttered to the floor. I stood in a tunica so sheer you could see my subligaculum, barely concealing the outlines of my manhood. The garment was so thin, I shivered.

"Oh, dear. You are cold," said the Emperor. "You see, our host, Marcus Julius Vestinus Atticus, though an esteemed general, is a bit of a fuddy-duddy when it comes to modern comforts. Everyone else in our stratum of society has at least *some* kind of central heating these days, even it's just two slaves fanning a furnace in the basement. But comfort's not a *Roman* virtue, is it, Atticus?"

"I think not, Caesar," said Atticus. I noted he didn't call him *Divinitas* as was now the fashion among Imperial flatterers. "A cold night in the German forest with only a pair of caligae and a tattered cloak, that's how a real soldier lives."

"Who needs a cloak, even? Some barbarian wench, or the chieftain's son, perhaps, just as warming, particularly if they struggle."

Atticus laughed, until he noticed that the Emperor was not.

"Sporus," said the Emperor, "come sit here. Statilia and I will keep you warm."

"I would not want to take the general's place at the head of the table," I said.

"He was just leaving," said the Emperor.

At which point, the tribune pulled a document out and began to read.

"In the name of Nero Claudius Caesar Augustus Germanicus, Pater Patriae, Pontifex Maximus—"

"You can skip the titles, Gerellanus, we haven't got all night," said Nero Claudius Caesar Augustus Germanicus.

"Marcus Julius Vestinus Atticus, you are under arrest for your part in the conspiracy of Piso to topple the monarchy."

At which point, Atticus laughed again, and this time, he got the joke. If you could call it a joke. "Couldn't you people have thought of a better excuse?" he said. "I'm old-fashioned. The Emperor may be a fool, but I don't break loyalty oaths. I'm a Roman."

The Emperor nodded. Then he motioned to me and I came close; he dandled me on his lap. "You've done me many favors, Atticus; now I'll do you a favor as well. You can be a Roman to the end. We're friends, so I'll let you commit suicide."

"Thank you, Caesar," said the general, and kissed the Divine Hand. He managed to make humility sound like vitriol. With an admirable show of dignity, he rose — and I slid into his seat, becoming the involuntary host and head of the table — and left the room, followed by two slaves, perhaps his personal body slaves.

"He hasn't even touched his flamingo pie," Statilia said at last. "It's his favorite."

She broke off a piece and popped it into my mouth.

It was, I admitted, succulent and smooth. The tongues, marinated in honey and a touch of garum, slithered between my cheeks until I washed them down with a white wine that had a pungent reek of Aleppo pine resin.

Statilia whispered to me, "Whatever you did, Sporus, it seems to have had the desired effect."

"Did you have to kill off the husband, Lucius?" I said into the Divinity's ear.

Statilia, who must have had very sharp hearing, said, "Oh, how deliciously topsy-turvy — the slave calling the God by his given name! It's like Saturnalia all year round."

"I'm free," I said.

"Indeed," she said, as though it were of no import. Why would it be? She had what she wanted, and needed no more favors from me.

"Can we have some more Alcaeus?" said the Emperor.

At that the singer, who had been simply standing there, occasionally undulating in a provocative way so as not to be completely ignored, struck up her lyre again and sang:

O Nicander! Your legs
are getting hairy;
beware lest it happen to your buttocks too
for then you shall know how rare it is
to find true love....

"Saucy!" said the Divinitas, patting the sheer silk about my thighs. "Well, we shan't let such a disaster befall you, shall we?"

I pretended to laugh, and took another bite of the pie.

Statilia snatched the rest out of my hand. "Not too much," she said. "You don't want to get fat, either."

The dinner was slowly returning to normal, if you could call flamingoes and suicide normal. Statilia and the Emperor kissed, using me the way you would use a silk cushion stuffed with the softest down, wrapping themselves around me, leaning into me ... it was good, though, to be a mere object. I sent my mind far away. I thought of the sea, the rhythm and the salt tang of the waves as they brought me to this bewildering land.

Presently, as the bawdy song came to an end, the tribune Gerellanus came and whispered in the Emperor's ear.

He held up his hand for silence. "It would appear," he said, "that the Lady Statilia Messalina is no longer married."

Some of the guests took on expressions of shock and horror. Everyone knew that Atticus's probity was beyond question and that he probably had had nothing to do with the Pisonian conspiracy, which by now was a tired old scandal anyway. But, perhaps, some of them *were* guilty. What if they were next?

"You'll need a husband," said the Emperor. "It might as well be me."

They must have been awaiting the cue all evening, because in an instant, the triclinium filled up with all the ready-made trappings of a wedding. There was a priest. There were children strewing nuts to symbolize fertility. There was an orchestra, and much pounding of drums and tooting of double flutes.

The Vestalis Maxima, who had not said a word during the dining, the singing, or the announcement of treason, rose and walked over to the main dinner table to preside over the marriage vows.

"Ubi tu Gaius, ego Gaia," she said, so that Statilia could repeat the words, a simple message that has been said a million times over eight centuries of Roman history, through the early monarchy, through the republic, through to now, modern times, the Empire.

But Nero could not wait for the vows to finish.

"We shall go now," he said, taking Statilia by the hand. "Gods do not need a ceremony to legalize their mating."

Abruptly, the guests, slaves, and hangers-on all started to shout, "Feliciter! Feliciter!"

Nero said to Gerellanus, "Get the body out first. Fresh blood makes a poor lubricant."

So saying, he led Statilia to the door of the triclinium, leaving chaos and confusion in his wake. At the doorway he stopped and looked straight at me. "Thank you, Sporus, for doing such a good job at the head of the table, keeping the wine flowing and the food coming."

Right, I thought. I stood up. Desperately trying to find something to say, I started off with, "Friends, don't go home yet. We don't want to waste the bounty of Atticus." I sounded like a fool. Then soldiers moved in to block all the possible exits, and an enormous roast pig, garnished with swans' wings, was carried in on the shoulders of four muscular Nubians.

"Whatever else we may say about him, Atticus certainly owned a good chef," I said, and my words were greeted with nervous applause.

"Excellent, my boy!" the Emperor shouted. Then, almost as an afterthought, "Oh, Sporus — you can have the house. Statilia won't be needing it."

He left the room, and soldiers closed ranks. The guests were not going to get to go home just yet. Not without finishing their dinner.

As soon as the Emperor seemed to have gone out of earshot, the gossip began. I found myself being bombarded with questions, though I knew nothing. One senator asked whether we were all going to have to commit suicide tonight. There were a lot of grim jokes after that, but I thought the food tasted particularly fine as well, and not just because most the guests assumed they would be slaughtered once the Emperor had sated his desires. The wine-slaves made their rounds more and more often.

Delicati wandered about, but few took advantage of them. There was too much anxiety in the air. There was a brief distraction when Croesus came into the room with a document he wanted me to put my name to. *"Now,"* he whispered urgently, "before Himself changes his mind." Apparently, I did own this house now. And it was bigger than Petronius's, though far less tasteful. I offered him wine, but he slipped away.

In the end, many of them were dozing off; only the old Vestal Virgin seemed wide awake, sullenly sipping her snow-cooled wine.

Even the music became sporadic. The singer had, perhaps, run out of the odes of Alcaeus. She was snoring in a corner, her arms wrapped around a pedestal on which sat a bust of Augustus.

The silence continued.

I too had had my share of wine, and I had not eaten much. Statilia's warning about not getting too fat was making me nervous.

I remember now how Hyacinth had fussed endlessly about his appearance, and keeping his looks.

Suddenly, an almost bestial shriek rent the stillness. A cry of desolation and despair. Like a child who has lost its mother, only it was the voice of —

"Sporus! Sporus!"

I straightened my tunica and stepped gingerly over the drunken senators. The soldiers parted for me. The screams were coming from an upper room.

"Sporus! I want you now!"

When a God summons you, there's nothing for it. You go, blindly, unthinking.

XXX

FORGING AN ALLIANCE

A good steward knows everything, senses exactly what is happening. Croesus had known to get the title to the general's property in writing, and now he stood at the foot of the stairs, holding the stola that would change me from Sporus to Poppaea.

The Emperor's screams were if anything more insistent. I followed the sounds and stepped into a luxurious bedchamber, the only room in the house that was not spare. Here, there were spoils of war; displays of enemy armor and weapons, a sculpture of Atticus himself, with his foot on the neck of some barbarian, at the foot of the couch so that the first thing the general would gaze on in the morning was the sight of his own victory.

The general had been discreetly removed, but there was blood on the floor, and a sword, too, that had not been cleaned yet.

On the bed lay Statilia Messalina. I thought for a moment he had killed her; but no, she was just exhausted from his depredations, and a little bruised, and moaning a little. Sitting beside her was the Divine Nero, undressed and still shrieking out my name.

"I'm here, Lucius," I said.

Abruptly, he stopped screaming.

"Have I been bad?" he said.

"Of course not, Divinitas," I said.

"No, no, that's not how we play this!" he said, pouting.

"Yes. You've been bad."

"Sterner!"

"Bad! Bad!"

"Am I a naughty Emperor?"

I was not sure how to feel ... sickened? embarrassed? compassionate? "Yes you are," I said softly. "Very naughty."

"You're not very good at this," he said at last. "The real Poppaea would have ... but you saw what happened to her."

I realized at last that while for Himself it was a game of whimsy, for me it could mean life or death. I put on what I imagined to be my most Agrippina-like voice. "Lucius Domitius!" I spat. "Nothing good will come of all this debauchery!"

"Oh, I know it, Mother," he said. "You'll have to beat me, I think."

"With what?" I said, in a parody of savagery. *"What?"*

Then I saw the bloody sword on the floor. It had a heft to it. Using the flat so I wouldn't drawn any Divine Blood, I had a crack at the Imperial buttocks. He screamed and I was taken aback before realizing that there was pleasure in his screaming. I took a few more blows. Once, I turned the sword at the wrong angle.

"One more of those, and I'll have you crucified," the Emperor gasped. And once again, in a small voice … "I'm sorry, I'm so sorry."

I wielded the sword with a little more care now. That had been a near disaster.

I looked over at Statilia Messalina, who was no longer shriveled in a corner of the bed. In fact, she seemed to have recovered completely. She was watching me intently. She had the hint of a smile. She was enjoying this, and, to my own self-disgust, so was I.

This little stint of play-acting was brief, however, for Tigellinus burst into the room. I tried to make myself disappear. Statilia sat up, and despite being naked, appeared suddenly dignified, even matronly.

"Divinitas," Tigellinus said, completely ignoring the spectacle before him, "General Vespasian is here."

"I thought we sent him to Judaea."

"You decided that only days ago, Divinitas. I believe he is here to discuss strategy."

"What strategy? Just crucify them."

"Lucius," I whispered, "you might not want to crucify an entire people."

"If they all had one neck between them," said the Emperor, "I'd snap it."

I had heard him say that many times.

"I'll meet him," he said. "Let me put on some clothes."

"Divinitas, there is also the matter of the guests at the banquet …."

"What? They haven't left yet?"

"You told us to detain them. Shall we just kill them?"

"Yes," he said. "Oh. General Vespasian will probably think it's wicked of me."

"Naughty!" I hissed in his ear, lifting the sword-hilt I'd been beating him with. He seemed to come to his senses, and allowed himself to be led out of the room, after throwing on a bloody toga that Atticus must have worn when he committed suicide.

"Come down when you're dressed," he said to me and Statilia. "I want to be seen with my beautiful wives."

I looked at Statilia as he left the room. We heard him padding down the marble steps in his bare feet.

Statilia said, *"Wives?"*

I said, "He's confused, Lady Statilia. You're his only wife … as of this evening, anyway."

"Let me be quite clear with you, you uppity little libertus," she said. "As of today, I am Imperatrix. And I have the blood of Imperatrices. The Divine Claudius's last Empress was also a Messalina. You are nothing."

"I know, Divinitas," I said, trying to sound humble. For I knew that she knew I could stand in her way if I wanted to. I was nobody, but I could be a nuisance. But it was best to be disingenuous.

"I don't mind where the God puts his mentula for the night," she said — the word sounded quite vulgar on her lips — "but you must acknowledge me as Imperatrix, no matter what silly games he chooses to play. There must only be one Imperatrix. You are to understand this at all times, or I'll have you raped by hyenas in the arena."

Then she started laughing, and I did too. We had both, after all, seen our Lord and Master at his most vulnerable. It was to be a détente of sorts, if an uneasy one.

"Of course, Divinitas," I murmured.

"In that case, let me help you get dressed. A shapeless stola as a coverall is not going to impress any of the arbiters of taste at court."

"But the only real arbiter is dead," I said, reminded suddenly of Petronius.

"True. I admired Petronius, too, you know. All the more reason to abandon simplicity and elegance, and go for the vulgar," she said. "It's the way of things. Oh, well done getting the house. I won't be needing it, of course."

"It was an afterthought, really," I said.

"I never liked it. Atticus was a peasant at heart, and my dowry alone could have bought ten of these."

Thus, alliance forged, we went down to meet General Vespasian.

XXXI

TITUS FLAVIUS VESPASIANUS

This house — which was now my house, including all its contents, both animate and inanimate, as I could see from the way that Croesus was ordering the slaves about in my name — had been miraculously tidied in a matter of minutes. An army of slaves must have been at work. There wasn't a vomit stain or an ostrich bone anywhere, and the busts and columns had been polished to shining.

The dining room was full again, but not with dinner guests. I stood beside Statilia. We had come to the conclusion that none of her clothes would fit me — for she was both statuesque and steatopygous, and I am slender, looking younger even than my tender age. So after trying on everything in she had handy, in the end I was wearing only the translucent tunica I had brought with me.

"Did the guests get killed?" I whispered to Statilia.

But a centurion standing nearby said, "It would have made more mess, so we let them shuffle home." One guest was still there, the head Vestal Virgin. I remembered that the Divinitas had called her "great-aunt" when we were at the trial of Rubria. Vestals are inviolate, unless they sleep around, so I suppose she never felt herself in any danger.

She sat at the dining couches alone, munching on bread and salt.

The Divinitas was seated on a curule in front of the dining area. To his left were a group of soldiers, including a man who I guessed immediately must be Vespasian. He was jowly, grizzled, gruff. To the Emperor's right were a wholly different assemblage. They were dancers, flower-arrangers, and a man wearing more gold ornaments than an Egyptian princess. This crowd was jostling for attention, being managed by a very beleaguered Epaphroditus, with the limping philosopher lad, Epictetus, taking notes by his side.

Himself was listening to the crowd on his right, while Vespasian's group was trying to distract him. "We'll have games of course," said Nero, "but especially chariot races. I am going to compete personally you know. And I will win the crown for my lovely … wife."

Nero saw me and Statilia. He held up his hand. He spoke of his new wife, but his eyes were on me.

"Greet the new Imperatrix," he said. A chorus of *aves* ran round the room. "My dear," he said to Statilia, "I've had these people brought in to organize the celebrations of our wedding and your elevation to the title of Augusta."

Statilia squeezed my hand. I daresay she had not expected *Augusta* quite so soon.

"Games, I think," said the Emperor, "very important games.

Titus Flavius Vespasianus cleared his throat. "Caesar, with the respect to the Judaean question—"

"Yes, yes, Vespasian," said Himself. "You'll do to the Jews what you did to the Britons, no doubt."

"Hardly, Sire," said the general. "The Britons are a loose confederation of disorganized tribes who hate each other as much as they hate us. They're separated by water from even their own kind, the Celts of the continent, who have mostly come to appreciate the gift of Roman civilization. Whereas in Judaea—"

"Judaea is a tiny, recalcitrant pimple on the flesh of Rome," said Nero. "She's a speck, surrounded by Rome. Why can you not engulf her?" He turned to a man who appeared to be the Editor of the games. "A hundred pairs, I think. And a Naumachia. Can we reenact the Aeschylus's *The Persians?*"

"Jupiter, Divinitas!" said the Editor. "There aren't enough condemned criminals to stage a battle that big. We've even run out of Chrestianoi."

"Perhaps we can buy a few," said Statilia.

"Meanwhile," said Vespasian, "I too need funds. To subjugate a people as unruly as these, as thoroughly as you have commanded …"

"There's always taxation," Statilia said.

"There's already tax on everything," Epaphroditus protested. "The people say you've taxed everything except their piss."

"Piss?" said the Emperor. "Sporus, didn't you mention a urine tax to me once?"

I kept silent. I *had* mentioned it to him once, and it was half in jest. I was surprised he recalled it. It had been an eventful day and night. But then, Himself had a sharp mind. Not an entirely sane one, but he didn't forget things. How could I have been so stupid?

Tigellinus spoke up, "I do recall, Divinitas."

"It's quite poetic, really. Rome's piss will feed her troops. It has a kind of mad logic to it."

"Caesar," Vespasian interrupted again, "these people are fanatics. They'll die for their God."

"Well," said the Emperor, "I *am* their God."

He had become exceedingly bored with the general. Presently, he told his spectacle planners he was going to go right now, to the Circus Maximus, to see for himself how the celebration of his new wedding should be carried out.

"Statilia," he said, "make sure that the General gets what he wants."

"Perhaps a little breakfast?" said General Vespasian.

Nero snapped his fingers. And the room was emptied of all the organizers, their attendants and *their* attendants. Only the Chief Vestal remained, still picking at her piece of bread.

It did not escape me that Vespasian had been eyeing me with some interest, even as he was describing the hardships of dealing with an intractable desert people and their vengeful god.

***

So you met General Vespasian! Gruff and grizzled, you called him! Did you make eyes at him, did you seduce him with your sensual voice? Did you sit on his lap in your sheer tunica?

I did not know what to think at all. I was confused.

You should have, you know. We hear that the General is on the march. If he arrives in Rome and dispatches the current Divinitas ... you might have staved off your fate. We've already had three Emperors this year — and a few would-be Emperors as well. People in the drinking-houses are saying, "This might be the one who sticks."

I had an inkling. It was when slaves started to bring in the refreshments....

***

Statilia and I took our places at the head couch, while the general went to use the latrina. The Chief Vestal was still seated, at our left this time.

Statilia said softly to me: "Watch this one. There's money on him to be the next Divinitas."

"He doesn't interest you? I know you are planning to survive *our* Divinitas."

"That will be hard enough," she said, "but I have plans beyond Nero. And this one obviously likes boys; he is a career soldier, and soldiers are not allowed to marry, you know."

The Vestal cackled. "If Lucius but knew the treason you're plotting!" she said. "But I don't care. Rubria was the last straw. He defiled one of us, and forced us to kill her. Rubria was very popular amongst the sisters, if you know what I mean."

General Vespasian returned. He sat down and was served wine and bread. A simple repast for a man of simple tastes.

Statilia said, "You must come to the games, General, before you head off to crush the rebellion."

"I don't care much for fake battles," he said. "War is a nasty business and watching condemned prisoners kill each other isn't much of a sport."

"But there will be a hundred matched pairs of gladiators as well," Statilia said. "Surely one such as you can appreciate the finer points."

"The Circus Maximus is not the ideal place to watch a proper gladiatorial match," he said. "Perhaps when I retire, I'll build a better venue. If I can find the funds. The spoils of a Judaean war might be what it takes. So … I'd best set sail for Judaea as quickly as possible."

"But Sporus will watch the games with you," she said. "And the Divinitas won't be sitting in the Imperial Box. You heard him. He's going to be in the chariot races. *In* them!"

"Himself?"

"Shocking, isn't it?" said the Vestalis Maxima. "The man has gone from being the Rome's great hope to Rome's great buffoon."

"Whose boy is this, Statilia, yours?" Vespasian said.

"He's a libertus, General," said Statilia. "And spoken for by High Olympus itself."

"Any mortal can attain Olympus," Vespasian said, "with enough legions." He looked at me appraisingly. "Celt?"

"I don't know what I am, General," I said. "But I'm told it's beyond Rome's edge."

"Exotic." He turned to Statilia. "His Greek's perfect, though."

"Eukharistô," I said.

"So you'll be there?" Vespasian said, carefully putting a hand on my knee. It was gnarled, but not unaffectionate.

I managed a smile. Even Nero's death, it seemed, might not end what I had become.

XXXII

MORS ...

First, it occurred to me that I should go home. Then, it occurred to me that I *was* home. The Divinitas, the newly minted Empress, and all the retinue, as well as Vespasian and all *his* retinue, had all left. Statilia had not seemed at all to want to remain; indeed, her clothes and precious belongings had been packed for days, I discovered.

In cataloguing Atticus's property, which was very efficiently done in a few large scrolls, almost as though Atticus assumed he was not long for this world — Croesus discovered that I was in fact, much richer than before.

I had an estate in Antium, a town house in Pompeii, and the income from a series of latifundia in Sicily where thousands of slaves worked the land, and where Atticus himself had never set foot in a decade.

As I have said, this house was expansive, though sparsely furnished. I could choose to live here or return to

Petronius's, whose house in the city strictly belonged to Marcus Vinicius but which was to all intents and purposes mine as well. Or I could remake this house in my own image.

Except I had no image. Or rather, I had many images, having being created many times out of the potter's clay of others' imaginations and desires.

"Croesus," I said, "It is really you who should take possession of our patronus's home, managing in for Marcus Vinicius."

"You'll need a steward here, too," he said.

"Why not Spider?" I said. "And we'll send for those who are close to me, starting with Hylas and Simon." Croesus despatched one of my new slaves to Petronius's immediately.

"You may want to sell off some of the household," Croesus said.

"I'll just free a few," I said. "That way I'll be a patronus in my own right." The next hour was spent introducing me to my property: cooks, body-slaves, dressers, wine-pourers, even a token delicatus, although Atticus's sexual taste did not run to much beyond straightlaced uxoriousness.

It was afternoon by the time Hylas arrived. When he saw me, he embraced me passionately. My new slaves eyed him cautiously, wondering whether, as my favorite, he would have the authority to bully them or have them scourged for no reason.

"Something awful has happened," he told me. "Simon's vanished."

"Run away?" That did not seem like him.

"Should I give his description to the vigiles?" Croesus said.

"No," I said, "I don't want him hounded by slave-catchers."

To imagine this child branded on the forehead with the mark of *fugitivus* was too much. Surely he had a reason to disappear.

"Do you think he went to find his brother?"

"He did, domine," Hylas said, "but he only took a couple of loaves. Something must have happened to him."

Although my sojourn with a group of Chrestianoi had suggested to me that they did not eat children or practice bloody rituals, one could never be sure with cults. The entire love-feast might have been put on to pull the wool over my eyes. Wildly, I imagined Simon being sacrificed to some barbaric deity. Hadn't Vespasian told us the Jews were fanatics? And weren't these people some kind of breakaway sect, even weirder than the Jews?

"Croesus," I said, "send some of our own people to make inquiries. But discreetly. In fact ... tell Marcus. A slave is a trivial matter for someone like him, but he was moulded by his uncle, and doesn't completely ignore the downtrodden. He can pull more strings than any of us."

Marcus was a good man. I had even been in love with him for a day or so, when he saved my life, so long ago.

So we spent the next few days moving my things into the big new house and watching Statilia Messalina's chests of belongings get carted away. Statilia herself I did not see; I assumed she was planning the festivities with Himself. I spent my days being briefed about my newfound wealth, or buying silly knickknacks in the Forum, and sometimes at the Baths. The newer Thermae Neronis were even bigger than the Baths of Agrippa, though they were in the Campus Martius and further away from my new residence, but they were a spectacle to marvel at, with entertainers, masseurs, and impressive works of art, and a library where I was able to read the poets those around me were always quoting.

It was true, I realized, that the spirit of poesy was dying. For in his haste to attain supremacy, Nero had managed to rid the world of some of its greatest wordsmiths. Seneca and Lucan were gone, and Petronius, of course, who had provided a kind of check on Himself's more self-indulgent fancies.

There was no news about Simon. I hoped that he'd found some connection to his brother. I did not imagine him being taken in by those cultists, but then again, for the sake of Adam, he may have chosen to be among them. To stop myself from worrying, I pretended not to have cared for him too much.

In a few days, a new series of games would begin. Although my mind was seething with confusion, I would have to stay calm. I did not want to draw attention away from the new bride, yet I had to be there. It would be best to go as a boy. But I should not look like a libertus. I should look like a prince. I should look worthy of the tales of my origins that had been circulating since I was first offered for sale.

***

How do you feel about the games now, now that you have a role to play?

Rome has built monuments to last a thousand years. Its armies have ground entire nations into oblivion. But to see

Rome at its most impressive, you have to look at the games. The resources of the entire world are poured into the games. Years of training gladiators. Tens of thousands of animals from every corner of the Empire. Thousands of prisoners and other societal dregs kept as fodder for the slaughter. The amazing efficiency of getting all of it fit together, with meticulous timing, an infrastructure as complex as running an entire kingdom, hundreds of freedmen and slaves to handle every detail, and all of this expended in the name of entertainment.

And I've always had a role to play in the games.

Just not this *role.*

Just not this one.

***

I arrived early, just before the midday break. I arrived in style, spending some of my new found wealth on a more ostentatious litter and exotic, matched litter-bearers — all Germans, with shaggy blond hair, with the skins of animals thrown over their shoulders and wearing nothing but gilded loincloths. Petronius would have laughed — it was the sort of vulgar conveyance that an ex-slave millionaire like Trimalchio, from the *Satyricon,* would have possessed.

I arrived with a small military escort organized by Marcus Vinicius.

When I arrived in the Imperial Box, I got my own round of applause. I was almost the only one there. I could only see Vespasian, in military regalia, and one or two senators and their attendants.

No one comes to the games during lunch-time. Most people don't want to see routine executions, so they are scheduled for the slowest and hottest time of the day.

I could not very well have a huge retinue in the Imperial Box but one attendant seemed mandatory, so I only took Hylas, dressing him almost as magnificently as myself.

I sat just below where the Emperor and Empress would be. The only other person occupying that tier was the Editor of the games, whom I had seen planning the event with the Emperor. Behind him stood Marcus.

No one shooed me to a lowlier seat, so I presumed I was where I should be. Presently, the King of Armenia showed up just as they were bringing on the andabatae. Tiridates sat next to me, one place further from the Imperial Seat.

"I know," he said. "I shouldn't still be here. Now that the Emperor has properly crowned me, I should go back to dealing with our own problems at home. But Rome ... you have to love this place. It's filthy, sprawling, chaotic, and full of entertainments like these. Look at the andabatae down there ... it's a ridiculous idea and only a mad genius could dream it up."

There were about twenty of them down there, ignominiously clothed in just their subligacula. They swung at the air guided only by sound, their flailing blows subjected to jeers and taunts.

"It's pathetic," I said.

One man pretended to be dead, and attendants came in, poking him with red-hot irons to see if he was faking. The man screamed. Tiridates giggled. Even Hylas smiled. They could find it amusing, because these criminals were not seen as human in any way. They were thieves, forgers, murderers.

"This is boring," Vespasian said. I am sure he was itching to return to the Judaean front and was there only to be seen by the Emperor. And perhaps to get a close peek at me, too.

When one lucky andabata decapitated another with a single blow, the crowd cheered and some even started calling for his freedom, and gasped in unison when another andabata swerved and spiralled into his space, gutting him.

Tiridates clapped. Hylas fetched us wine.

"I would have left, but I promised the Divinitas I'd watch him race," Tiridates said.

The andabatae were all dead and it was time for damnatio ad bestias. The bodies were dragged off and other doors opened. It was the Chrestianoi, and indeed, the organizers were right; it was a sad selection indeed. The last time I had been at the ludi, there were so many to be eaten that it almost upset the day's schedule. This time the lions would make quick work of it.

Suddenly, Hylas gripped my foot and pointed. It was then that I saw that, among the at most two dozen victims, leading the sad procession, was Viridian. And that in the group was Adam. And beside him was Simon.

I stood up, turned to Marcus. "There's some kind of mistake. That's my slave."

Marcus Vinicius stepped down and said, softly, "The one who ran away?"

"Yes. And there is his brother. And there's Seneca's freedman. Please … can we save them?"

"Any other time," Marcus said. "But now … now is not the time. You can defy the law, the senate, even the gods. But not Rome. And all around us is Rome. Rome is watching you, Sporus. All of Rome. We are her slaves. Even Nero."

"What aren't you telling me, Hylas?" I said.

Hylas began to weep. "While you were away … he came back to say goodbye to us."

"He bought into that whole charade?"

"Slap him, Sporus," Marcus whispered.

"Why?"

"You're a dominus. People have to see that you can control your own slaves."

"Do it, domine," Hylas said. "These people must respect you."

I slapped him, harder than I intended, because he wailed. Those in the Imperial Box nodded approvingly, seeing that I knew my proper rank in society. He crouched down low and hugged my feet. "He is my friend, too," I said softly. "But this is the Imperial Box." Louder, I said, "Wipe your tears, slave."

They were herding the captives out to the middle of the arena. I saw Simon and his brother hold hands. Reaching into his tunica, Hylas handed me a small scrap of a scroll. He said, "He left this for you. I can't read it." On it, Simon had written:

I love you, domine. You know why I am doing this. It isn't because I believe the nonsense these people preached to me. You understand me. Our sacred writings say (the letter continued in Greek) *Pos aisomen ten oden Kyriou epi ges allotrias? I will still love you when I am in the next world.*

What had Simon meant by "How can I sing the song of the dominus in a strange land?" I had never asked him to sing. Or did he mean by *kyrios* some kind of non-earthly lord, some God? Had Vespasian been right when he explained that these were an intractable, incomprehensible people? Had Simon become one of the Chrestianoi, or was he merely looking for a way to commit suicide?

I would never know. And here, I dared not speak to anyone about it. I put away the note.

Rome was watching.

And I was the mirror of Rome. I was becoming like them. The games are supposed to teach Roman virtues, manly virtues: to be inured to the sight of bloodshed, to laugh at pain, to stay stalwart in the face of death. Yes, this was not the first time I'd seen people being eaten. Hylas closed his eyes. I forced myself to look.

"I'm Roman, too, now," I told myself. My eyes welled up, but I would not let the tears come.

XXXIII

ET TRIBUTUM …

I watched all of it, until the bestiarii came with spears, on horseback and in chariots, to hunt and kill the lions, to finish off the predators who had just feasted on my friends.

Hylas did not watch. His eyes were closed. But he heard it all, which might have been worse.

I had not even had a moment for private thoughts. As the last lion was dragged away, the Lady Statilia Messalina entered the Box, all white and gold — even her face, painted in layers of lead and gilt. She was escorted by naked young Nubians, each holding a corner of a billowing cloak, which covered her completely and fluttered behind her in a flurry of wind created by braided Germans wielding peacock-feather fans.

Another fanfare! In a dramatic gesture, the Nubians unwrapped Statilia's white and gold cloak, revealing that beneath it she was dressed entirely in green!

The applause was thunderous, especially from those of the public who favored the green faction. She was so dazzling that few noticed the slaves sweeping the blood from the sand below.

She billowed down the steps and took her royal seat. She nodded towards me. There was more applause; the crowd was acknowledging the fact that I held the favor of the God.

A water-organ began to play, and bucinae blew deafeningly from every corner of the Circus. From the far end, the chariots made their processional entry. The crowd was chanting the names of their favorite riders and the colors of their faction.

Finally there came Nero.

There was a gasp. Not just because the God had lowered himself to the vulgar occupation of chariot driver. He had already done that by singing and acting in public.

He was driving a chariot with ten horses. Ten pure white horses, caparisoned in gold and green. *Ten!*

"Can he do that?" Tiridates said, laughing. "Audacity!"

"The rules do specify *four* horses," said one of the senators.

"Gods don't have rules," Statilia said.

For a moment, the crowd had fallen silent. Have you ever heard a hundred thousand people catch their breath all the same time?

In that hush, Nero's chariot was approaching. He wore a green cloak which was continuously flapping in his face.He was having trouble controlling the ten horses — of course he was, those flimsy chariots are designed for lightness — and it was embarrassing to watch. But the people dared say nothing.

Until someone breached the silence, a lone cry —

"Down with the urine tax!"

Nero turned. He could not quite tell where it was coming from, but he pointed in its general direction, and suddenly a detachment of soldiers could be seen rushing through the aisles towards the cry.

Then there came another, from a different part of the Circus. And another.

They were all shouting with the same enthusiasm as when they had cheered before. The Divinitas managed to get the ten horses to move forward in a more or less straight line. He moved towards the Imperial Box, ignoring the crowd, but the shouting was like thunder now.

And then I felt it. A splash on my face, then another.

People were urinating off the sides of the tiers. Jeering, hooting, and pissing. Statilia Messalina acted outraged, but she seemed to be enjoying it as well. The chorus became a rhythmic, pounding ostinato of "No urine tax! No urine tax!"

It was impossible to control them. Soldiers marched about, lashing a few of them. But they were in an ugly mood and the soldiers were simply too few. The arena was filled to capacity, and no one was prepared for a riot.

Nero handed the reins to a professional charioteer, who urged on the horses through to the Box. As he came closer I could see his enraged expression.

Vespasian said, "This might be a good time to go to Judaea."

The shouts died down, as more soldiers filled the stands. The silence of a hundred thousand people was as terrifying as their chanting.

Himself, Master of the Known World, looked undignified as the ten-horse chariot pulled right up to the Box. I could see his expression clearly now. It was not rage exactly — I knew well how the Divinitas looked when he was angry. It had set into a mask, almost emotionless. It was when Nero put on this face that he was furthest removed from reality.

"It is for you I ride, my mistress, my wife, my mother," he said, but he did not look up at Statilia. He seemed to be looking at me. Seeing Simon's death had sent my feelings fleeing deep into the back of my mind. Now, in addition to revulsion and grief, I felt stark terror as well.

Nero smiled. That was the most terrifying thing of all.

He made an ironic bow to the Editor of the Games. Then he turned to his Empress. But again, he looked straight at me.

"He can't very well salute himself," Statilia said.

He kept looking at me.

"Delicious!" said the King of Armenia. "He wants the *delicatus* to drop the handkerchief!" He tapped my shoulder. "Or should I say, the Prince of an Unknown Land?"

It was no good to say I was no delicatus. It was no good to say I was free. The Empress drew a piece of white silk from inside her stola and handed it to me. It smelled of perfume and femininity.

The chariots lined up, the Emperor's grotesque as his horses stretched far over the starting line. Statilia beckoned for me to come and sit beside her. Not on the thronelike sedilla of the God himself, but in her own chair, which was capacious enough. "We'll do it together," she said. She took my hand and lifted it in the air. The fabric fluttered and she turned to the Editor so he could signal the cornua, bucinae, and drums.

All at once the fanfare struck up. "Let go now!" she said. She beckoned to her slaves with the peacock fans. I let the cloth fly and the slaves fanned furiously so it flew out over the arena. Then I returned to my seat.

The chariots were off! Any urine tax protests were drowned now in the screams for the Reds, Blues, Whites and Greens. Nero's ten horses were immediately out of control, sprinting at different paces, dragging the chariot in a zigzag pattern — but the chaos was working as the sheer number of horses began overrunning the lanes and throwing the competition into confusion.

The crowd loved it! Every time one of the Emperor's horses reared up, whinnying, a thousand people whinnied in response. The Greens could not help but be in the lead because his horses were in everyone's way.

Afraid to be seen to overtake the Emperor, others lagged behind. "Cowards!" the audience yelled.

Presently one of the Blues managed to snake through the melée, leaving two overturned chariots in his wake. One lagging charioteer was already being dragged around by crazed horses.

The Divinitas's team was thrown in such confusion that they smashed into the Vestal Virgins' balcony as the crowd roared in shuddering delight.

The Emperor was dislodged now, clinging for dear life to the side of his chariot as it crashed! A detachment of cavalry forced its way into the arena, blocking off the area while slaves carried Nero away on a stretcher.

The crowd cheered! "Divinitas! Divinitas!" they shouted, seeming to have forgotten about the urine tax.

The race went on. I couldn't understand what was happening. It was even hard to see which lap had been reached, despite the display in the center island of the arena. By what seemed to be the sixth lap, the Circus was in disarray. Unharnessed horses roamed. A charioteer had an arm severed. The crowd shrieked in delight.

Eventually, a chariot seemed to have made it through the last lap. One of the Whites. The charioteer waved his arms to receive applause, but the audience was booing.

Then, suddenly, a huge cheer. Himself, the Master of the World, was being carried into the Imperial Box, propped up by a pair of hefty centurions. They managed to get him to his chair. Then they lifted him up and he spread out his arms.

The Editor read the judges' decision: Caesar had triumphed. He had won the first prize! The crowd was roaring at this absurdity.

A golden wreath was brought in on a pillow of green silk. The Editor did not dare to crown the Divinitas himself, but Statilia, smiling, placed the wreath on his head. He kissed her, acknowledging her before all Rome as Empress.

Exhausted by his injury and by all the excitement, Himself sank back into his chair, and signalled that the next event should begin. It was a bit of comic relief after the chariot race, giving them time to clean up the arena in time for another race — amazons fighting dwarfs.

Noticing me seated on the step below, the Emperor reached out and touched my head. I turned. He called me up to the throne and made me sit next to him. He put his arm around me.

"Did you enjoy my victory?" he whispered in my ear.

"You were stunning, Divinitas," I said.

"You know I cheated. You're the only one who would say so to my face, so don't lie to me."

"It did come as a surprise," I said.

He kissed me on the cheek. "We have to be here all day long, and then there's a farewell banquet for Vespasian and Tiridates. And after that, I shall have to perform my marital duties. But after *that....*"

"After that, Lucius?" I said sweetly.

"Look!" he pointed. "That amazon's tunic has been ripped off. They really do amputate one breast, just as in the legend."

"Fascinating," I said, snuggling up to him a little.

"After that, you'll come to me. The real you, Poppaea. In your true shape. I know, now the Senate elevated you to Olympus, so you can come to me in any form. It's good that you're a boy in public, because I'm married. But in the night...."

"I am whatever you make me," I said, "my dominus, my ruler, my God." How could I say otherwise? I lived in a world where those I loved committed suicide or were eaten by lions. I looked into his eyes, trying to show as little of my true self as possible. But in his eyes I saw only openness, only truth. In the deepest part of his soul, he saw me as Poppaea.

Which meant that I, who was named Sporus, but whose true name was known only to the dead, had no self left at all.

XXXIV

CAELUM...

I spent many hours in one of the Emperor's private baths. Hylas tended to me, scraping every inch of me with a strigil, oiling and re-oiling me with an olive oil scented with attar of roses that had come all the way from Parthia.

A little time with Hercules, because I knew that Poppaea always had, behind her fragrance, a pungent hint of a masculine feline odor.

More time with a makeup artist that Actë herself sent to me, trying to replicate the whiteness that Poppaea loved, only in the end to wipe it all off when the artist suggested that the Divinitas might prefer my natural smoothness.

By the time I went to the Imperial bedchamber, escorted by Hylas, it must have been the sixth hour — midnight.

In the corridor, I crossed paths with Statilia Messalina, who had a retinue of handmaidens, all with candles. She stopped when she saw me.

"You look perfect." she said.

"You too," I said.

Though, it must be said, Statilia Messalina looked as though she had been through storm and fire. Her hair was wild, her eyes were tired, her cheeks hollow.

"You flatter me. But I've done my duty," she said. "Now you must do yours."

"What *is* my duty?"

"I took care of his physical needs," she said. "But you alone must salve his psyche. But don't you fear. He's tired out. The chariot race — he was more wounded than he lets on. And he knows he didn't win. He's taken out all his rage, his sense of powerlessness, on me. Now, you'll find him gentle as a lamb."

I found Nero Claudius Caesar Augustus Germanicus alone and asleep. A lone oil lamp flickered in the gloom-steeped chamber. The doors to the secret garden were open but there was no moon, only starlight.

I went and sat beside the man I hated, despised, pitied, and yet in some way also loved. I was beautiful, I know I was. I, Sporus, was not Poppaea, but Poppaea lived within me. I remembered her dying moments. In my mind I could see her, wounded, at the gates of Heaven, demanding admittance because the Senate had proclaimed her a goddess. Did the immortals obey the Senate, or was this just one more human vanity?

I bent over the Emperor's face and kissed his lips.

My tears moistened his cheeks.

Slowly, he woke.

"You came," he said softly. "The only one who truly haunts my dreams."

He drew me into his arms.

How long could I continue this deception?

He caressed me, not just with his hands but with soft words. Not his own words, but words borrowed from the greatest poets of the past. "When I see you," he said, "my tongue falls silent ... a delicate flame rushes beneath my skin ... with my eyes I do not see, but my ears hum, I'm covered with sweat, I'm trembling, shaking ..."

Sappho, I thought. How well Petronius had taught me. And how soul-stirring, for the most powerful man in the world to make love to me with the words of the greatest poet who ever lived.

I melted into him then. Thoughts of Simon devoured by lions, of Spider in the hands of the torturer, of Rubria shrieking from the hollows of the earth ... yes, I had those thoughts, but a great ocean of passion rose up and swept away those mortal hurts. "Of all the children of heaven and earth," I whispered, "Love is the most precious." This I said to the man who had killed, maimed, destroyed all the people I ever loved. I said it and in that moment meant it.

The gentleness became a tempest. The God tore at the priceless silks and ripped them from me. I was afraid that now he would know I was not Poppaea, but he turned me over and took me from behind with such tenderness I felt no pain until, engorged, he made me cry out his name again and again and again ... "Lucius! Lucius!"

It was at this moment of climax that heaven turned to hell.

Nero let go of me and I fell, limp, onto the bed.

He sat up abruptly. He did not look at me as a lover now, but as a man looks at an insect.

"Your voice is changing, Sporus," he said. "The illusion will end."

In desperation, clinging to him, I cried out, "No, my love. It won't end. This moment will be forever. I'll *make* it last forever! Oh, Tata, Tata, I swear it, I swear it."

He took me in his arms again. "Forever? Do you swear it?"

"I do!" I cried, clutching him to me with such ferocity I felt my heart would break.

But the Emperor twisted away, sat up, called out the name of one of the slaves who were always present, in the shadows, invisible, until needed.

"You said I couldn't marry you," he said. "But I can."

XXXV

... ET INFERNUM

Two soldiers entered the room and took me away. I was stunned. I did not struggle. We went down, down, down, past the public areas of the palace, down rude stone steps, then more steps that were just packed earth, a dank place deep in the bowels of the building.

"Are you going to kill me?"

No answer. They brought me to a small room with a narrow bed, where a man stood, and behind him, rows and rows of sharp, gleaming metal instruments.

I knew why I was here.

Since that day I have tried to forget what happened.

The best surgeons in the world are still butchers, and castration is a fate meted out to slaves, so it is not normally an operation that is taken with much care. Perhaps this was the most gifted butcher in the world, brought in from

Greece or Egypt to attend to the needs of the Imperial household. Still, a butcher.

"You won't feel anything," he said, as they put me down on the bed.

They poured poppy juice down my throat, and followed it with wine laced with willow bark. They said it would dampen the feeling. There was so much fluid I felt I was drowning.

But I did not become unconscious.

Then they held me down.

I screamed until my throat was raw.

They strapped my legs to a rack that, I was sure, doubled as a torture device. They trussed me up tight, like a sacrificial animal. It took four Imperial guardsmen to hold me down.

When the surgeon began his work, the pain was unbearable, and I did pass out. I think, in a way, I died.

It certainly felt like death. Or what I have heard that death is like, the detachment of the self, the out-of-body feeling. I seemed to float into the air, and I watched what the surgeon was doing to me, watched myself lying there, and them thinking I was numbed from the poppy. The pain was still there, though it had been pushed far down into the pit of consciousness, like a horrifying childhood memory, gnawing, constant. As the knife started to tear flesh, my detached soul fled …

I floated.

Around me clouds scudded. I was carried on the breeze. The world beneath became small and distant. I could see all of Rome, a glittering mass of marble nesting in a sea of filth. Beyond Rome, I could see Vespasian at the head of his legions, thousands of men in an endless line marching down an impossibly straight road toward the harbor at Ostia.

Soaring higher, I saw the whole of the Mare Nostrum, the sea at the heart of the Empire. I saw our whole world. I saw Judaea in flames. I saw it all, just as you see me now, but with the eyes of a spirit. I saw the dark forests of Germany. I even saw the land I was born in, at the furthest edge of the known world. The wind was warm and I floated aimlessly in its embrace for a long time, I don't know how long.

At length a temple shimmered in the cloud-banks. I came to rest on a cushion of mist. There was no ground, but where I stood was soft and yielding. I found myself walking slowly toward the steps of the temple. Its roof rested on tall Ionic columns and was sculpted with a frieze of winged Cupids, and the frieze was alive, the images moved, the love-gods fluttered about and smiled down on me.

I walked along a straight Roman road, covered with gold dust and rose petals. On either side, children scattered more petals, crying "Feliciter! Feliciter!"

On the steps of the temple stood famed lovers from the stories of the Greeks. There was Hyacinth in the arms of Apollo — but it was *my* Hyacinth, and he was radiant. There too were Eros and Psyche, Hercules and Hylas — *my* Hylas — Leda and the Swan, even Persephone and Hades. And lovers of ancient and modern history — Harmodius and Aristogeiton, Hero and Leander, Alexander and Hephaestion, even Antony and Cleopatra. All were welcoming me, congratulating me, as I ascended the steps.

The marble was cool on my bare feet as I crossed from light into the temple's shade. Inside, the walls glowed with their own light.

I was dressed in bridal finery.

My husband waited for me at the altar of Jupiter. He was the Divine Nero, strumming on a kithara and filling the heavens with his rich voice.

Beside him stood Statilia Messalina, but she was garbed as a vestal virgin. And behind the altar, as tall as an entire building, was Jupiter Optimus Maximus. Even his breathing was the sound of distant thunder, and when he spoke, the stones of the temple trembled.

Say the words, the god thundered.

I spoke, and my words reverberated in the chamber:

Ubi tu Gaius, ego Gaia.

The Divinitas put down his kithara. He held out his arms to me and I took his hands in mine. The Emperor smiled and pulled me into an embrace. His body was warm. His love was real.

Then Jupiter Optimus Maximus spoke ...

And what will you sacrifice, child, to receive this pure, eternal love?

Statilia Messalina held out a knife.

It glistened.

She bore down on me and slashed into my flesh —

And then the pain came, clawing into me, consuming me, such pain, and I screamed and screamed and still the pain came, as though they were cutting away not just flesh, but selfhood, my past, my dreams, my hopes, my loves, ripping these things out of me ... and still I screamed until I reached a dark place, void of feeling.

I floated again. But not in the sunlight, not among the clouds. This was a place of nothingness. No sensation. In pushing away the pain I had also pushed away all sight, sound, feeling.

I don't know how long I drifted in that abyss.

Occasionally I thought I heard a voice. My mother, calling me by my secret name. Hyacinth, whispering "Domine, domine." But none of it was real.

But after a time that seemed forever, I smelled the sea.

I could feel motion. The waves. Wildly, I thought, *I have turned back time. I'm on the ship, in chains, starting my slave existence all over again. All that has happened has been a dream. Any moment now, that pirate is going to rape me back to consciousness.*

But that did not happen. The scent of the sea grew stronger. I was moving. I could hear, as from an infinite distance, the slap of oars, the cry of the hortator, the whip as an overseer lashed the galley slaves.

"Am I going home?" I murmured.

I heard someone's voice. "He's awake."

Gentle arms of a boy took me by the shoulders and raised me up, so I half-sat, leaning against soft cushions. I opened my eyes.

Sunlight. So dazzling I had to halfway close them again.

I groaned.

Then came the shouts of a dozen men, in disciplined, military unison: "Ave, Imperatrix! Ave, Imperatrix! Ave, Imperatrix!"

XXXVI

AVE, IMPERATRIX

And so you became, officially, an Empress of Rome. A living Goddess. It's an honor to prepare you for your last ceremonial act.

My memory is still unclear about the castration. When I try to remember I just see those dream-images. The wedding on Olympus, the famous lovers of myth and history, the children scattering flowers, the glint of the knife. After that there's an overwhelming pain, and a long, long nothingness.

And when you emerged from that nothingness you were on a ship, and soldiers were hailing you as Divine Empress?

It's hazy. But it's coming back to me....

***

I was on the upper deck of a trireme. Perhaps even a quinquereme. It was huge. The splash of the oars was louder, and we moved more steadily and smoothly, than the ship of my captivity. As I regained consciousness, they were still hailing me as Empress.

There were a hundred soldiers gathered around me, so this was definitely a quinquereme. Hylas crouched next to me, and fed me plain clear water from a silver cup.

"Am I going home?"

"Everywhere is home, Divinitas," Hylas said.

At length Croesus emerged from below. He saluted me with "Ave, Imperatrix," and helped me to sit up. Soldiers lifted me up and carried me to a chair where I could see the waves.

I asked Croesus where we were going, why they were all hailing me as Empress.

"You don't remember anything?" he said.

"No. Just floating in the clouds. Pain and then something numbing. And oblivion. A lot of oblivion."

"The Divinitas commanded that an impressive ceremony be held in the palace. There were senators. There were tribunes, consuls, vestal virgins, and feasting, three days of feasting. Statilia herself welcomed you as sister."

"Why don't I remember?"

"A lot of poppy juice. You were barely conscious, though you spoke quite a great deal, even sang along with the Divinitas. Odes of Sappho, I think."

"So the wedding I dreamed of ... it was true then. I spoke the words."

Croesus said, "Yes. You are Nero's wife, and we have been travelling for seven days ... we are already in the waters of the province of Graecia."

Greece....

I lifted the sheet that they had put over me. I was naked underneath it. I tried to reach for what used to belong to me. They had removed the testes completely. The stitching was finely done and it was healing, and they had not removed *everything* — I could still pee like a boy. But whether the roots of feeling were gone as well, whether I could still summon up any kind of passion, I had yet to find out.

"Divinitas," said Croesus, "you are the same person you always were."

"I'm not," I said. "If I were, you would not have addressed me as 'divinity,' would you?"

"Just an expression," said Croesus, "and used out of an abundance of caution. It's an order from the Master of the World, and not addressing you by royal titles is now punishable by death."

I said, "You are not to call me that, unless Himself is in earshot. And Hylas, not you, either."

At that moment, Nero's secretary Epaphroditus emerged. With him was the boy philosopher Epictetus, whose limp had grown noticeably worse. They both made much of me, feeding me a little broth, a little warmed wine. The sun climbed higher; a high wind sprang up, moist and warm. The drumbeat of the hortator eased a little as the quinquereme fed on the wind. But now and then, the lash still whistled from below, and the slaves still cried out in pain.

Epictetus said to me, "In Rome, all beautiful things derive from pain. The secret of survival is to make sure it's someone else's pain."

They covered me with a cloak of purple, the purple only permitted to royals. They sat me up straight. They put cushions behind me and beneath me so that despite my tiredness, I could take on an aura of divinity.

At length, Himself, Nero Claudius Caesar Augustus Germanicus, Father of the Country, Imperator, Supreme Pontiff, Master of the World, emerged from a pavilion curtained in purple silk.

The Emperor wore clothing thoroughly dipped in purple and bordered with gold thread. On his head he wore the golden wreath he had won despite being thrown from his ten-horse chariot.

Smiling, he came to me. He kissed me on the cheek.

"Purple becomes you," he said.

"Thank you, Lucius," I said.

He gestured expansively at the sea and quoted Aeschylus: "*Estin thálassa, tis de nin katasbései?*"

"There is the sea — and who shall drain it? — the sea that brings forth purple, more valuable than silver, ever fresh, with which we dye our clothes ..." I said.

Nero smiled.

"Where are we going?" I asked him.

"We are going where we can be ourselves," he said. "To the homeland of poetry and music. Where we can forget the odious work of governance, and live in the moment."

But wouldn't the Empire collapse? I thought.

Sensing my thoughts, Nero said, "Oh, I left Statilia behind as regent. She can repeal the urine tax, if she wants. She can do anything she wants."

"And Judaea?"

"Vespasian can kill every living creature in that forsaken land, for all I care. We're going *home,* my beloved. We'll celebrate the mysteries in Eleusis, the birthplace of Aeschylus. We'll see plays and hear fine poetry. And my work will be heard in the most discriminating competition of all time ... the Olympics."

"But Lucius," I said, "I don't think this year is an Olympiad year."

"They'll change it," he said, a twinkle in his eye. "Can you stand?"

I could, with a bit of help from Hylas. So I staggered up to portside, facing the shore. I leaned against the wooden wall and watched the distant land. The Emperor stood behind me, supporting me.

At that moment, he did not seem mad at all. He held me tenderly. The decision to go to Greece had reinvigorated him. "We'll leave it all behind us," he said. "When we celebrate the mysteries together, we will be reborn. I'll make new songs about you, your beauty, your wisdom. I will make you immortal. We'll have a new start."

I had not even had an *old* start yet, but I imagined he meant that he would have a second Poppaea now, a better Poppaea than the Poppaea he had kicked to death.

"You are the only one I love," he said softly, "Poppaea."

He left me then, and I found myself alone, leaning into the wind, having now lost everything that made me myself.

Yet I could not even weep. I had been emptied of all feeling. They had drained me of everything, and now they planned to refill me. I was only a wine-kylix, and they were going to choose what vintage to pour into me. I was a freedman who had lost even the fragment of freedom I had had as a slave.

Yet I had survived. Or at least, *someone*, living inside my body, had survived. The sea, sparkling in the sunlight, was achingly beautiful. The oars slapped in a slow rhythm beneath the whisper of the wind and cries of seabirds. Nowhere is the sky more blue than Greece.

Soon we would be at the birthplace of Aeschylus, father of the drama. And Aeschylus in his *Oresteia,* Sophocles in *Oedipus,* the great sage Solon, too, had all said the same thing: "Call no man happy until he is dead."

Yet I knew that in Eleusis, one would die and be reborn. That was the nature of the mysteries that were celebrated there.

But hadn't I died already? How many more times would I have to be emptied out and remade in another's image?

I prayed to the gods, but only the wind replied.

THANK YOU

Thank you so much for taking this journey with me into the story of Sporus, one of the most extraordinary figures in ancient history.

There is much more to the story: the tour of Greece, Nero's ignominious return to Rome and his death, and how Sporus survived the reigns of Galba and Otho only to be sentenced to die in the arena while playing the role of the goddess Persephone.

Reviews mean a lot. Thirty years ago, my books came out from traditional publishers like Simon & Schuster and Atheneum. Someone else took care of getting the books reviewed. But in my old age, the industry has changed. Now, I'm doing everything on my own. Reviews make a significant difference.

So, if you feel like it, please leave a review for the book especially if you purchased it on amazon. The link can be found here if you are a U.S. reader:

https://www.amazon.com/dp/B0C62LB2NM

and here for U.K. readers

https://www.amazon.co.uk/dp/B0C62LB2NM

If you can't wait to go on with the story, and have access to a U.S. Amazon account, check out Amazon Vella, where the third book is being serialized.

https://www.amazon.com/kindle-vella/episode/B09MR6789C

www.ingramcontent.com/pod-product-compliance
Lightning Source LLC
Chambersburg PA
CBHW020525310726
48979CB00014B/2219/J

* 9 7 8 1 9 4 0 9 9 9 8 8 3 *